THE POOR RICH

BY THE SAME AUTHOR

The Harlequin Edition

For Children

THE POOR RICH

Julian Fane

Book Guild Publishing
Sussex, England

First published in Great Britain in 2009 by
The Book Guild Ltd
Pavilion View
19 New Road
Brighton, BN1 1UF

Typesetting in Garamond by
Keyboard Services, Luton, Bedfordshire

Printed in Great Britain by
CPI Antony Rowe

A catalogue record for this book is available from
The British Library

ISBN 978 1 84624 292 2

First Chapter of Nine

English countryside near the market town of
Teasham. English summer weather, drizzle under
blankets of cloud. An English farmstead on an
English hillock. English rural landscape, nothing
untoward happening, a rook cawing in the middle
distance.

A road runs round the base of the hillock, a
B-road, and a track turns off it. The track, a
cart-track of yore, winds uphill to an isolated
farmhouse and farm buildings. Overgrown hedges
hide most of the track from view, but here and
there a rutted surface is visible. The fields on
either side are growing thistles, nettles, brambles
and saplings. Walls and fences have disintegrated.
There is no sign of life at the farm. An unusual
sequence of events begins.

A large black car is manoeuvring on to the
track and heading for the farm. It disturbs the
pigeons and other birds of the air who are
unaccustomed to traffic. The car stops, perhaps
stuck in a pothole. Nobody gets out, but windows
are opened and white urban faces look down at
the track and up at the farm. The driver and
passengers seem to be uncertain of where they
are and where they are going. The windows close.

The car revs, jerks forward, advances, swinging this way and that in order to avoid obstacles.

It comes to a halt in a yard, a farmyard, which looks more like a mud pie. A red brick farmhouse and a variety of dilapidated sheds stand on three sides of the yard. Some of the sheds are open-fronted, others have padlocked doors and broken windows.

The four men in the car stay put. The engine of the car is switched off. The driver opens his window and calls, 'Anyone about?' He calls again, louder – no answer. The ignition is switched on again, as if to suggest the visitors have decided to drive away, then off once more. A long silence is broken by the blare of the car's horn. The driver honks twice more.

Third time could be called lucky. A figure emerges from the recesses of one of the open-fronted sheds. It – he – is hardly human: bent, sloth-like, wearing an old sou'wester, an old mac with old sacking over its shoulders, a dirty flatcap and gumboots.

The driver of the car shouts through his window: 'Morning!'

The other's response sounds like clearing his throat.

The driver raises his voice. 'We're looking for Goose Farm.'

'Ar.'

'Is this Goose Farm?'

'What for?'

'I beg your pardon?'

'Why're you wanting to know?'

'You tell me first if this is Goose Farm.'

'Some say so.'

'Who are you?'

'Who are you, comes to that?'

'We want to talk to Mr S. Yockenthwaite.'

'Ar.'

'Does he live here?'

'That depends.'

'What does it depend on?'

'Whether I tell you.'

The old man turns his back on the car. The visitors step out, into the mud, and slosh towards the shed, shouting and gesticulating.

'Who are you?' the visitors demand in chorus.

'Mind your business,' the man retorts over his shoulder.

One visitor, older than the others and wearing the darkest suit, takes over.

'Listen, sir, if you will. We've come here to inform Mr Yockenthwaite of something to his advantage. Have we come to the right place?'

The old man has turned again.

'Could be,' he admits.

'Is Mr S. Yockenthwaite at home?'

'What's to his advantage?'

'I can't reveal that – it's not allowed. Please, sir, more information – is Mr Yockenthwaite alive?'

'Thinks he is.'

'He lives at Goose Farm – that's right, isn't it?'

'Right enough.'

'Could you tell him we have urgent and interesting news for him?'

'What's that?'

'Money's involved.'

'That so?'

'Is Mr Yockenthwaite available?'

'You got money for him?'

'Roughly speaking.'

'How much?'

'It's only a bit of paper that we have to put into Mr Yockenthwaite's hand.'

'You can hand it over.'

'I'm sorry – we don't know you – it's the farmer, Mr Yockenthwaite, we have to meet and talk to.'

'He's not about.'

'Where is he?'

'Indoors.'

'Thank you. We'll ring his doorbell.'

'Nar. He'll not hear no bell.'

'Why?'

'He's laid up.'

'Ill you mean?'

'He can't take no paper. I'm his deputy.'

'Deputy?'

'I do all the business round here.'

'Who are you, sir, if I may ask?'

'Cousin.'

'Mr Yockenthwaite's cousin?'

'I live with him.'

'Will he be up and about soon? We could come back tomorrow at a pinch.'

'Not he.'

'Why's that?'

'Bedridden and won't see nobody, 'cept me.'

'Can you identify yourself? Have you any means of identification?'

'Nar. I'm a Yockenthwaite. I can sign for parcels.'

'But are you Mr S. Yockenthwaite?'

'Sometimes they call me that.'

'What does the S stand for?'

'It's a Bible name.'

'Are you Mr Shadrach Yockenthwaite?'

'Could well be. Let's see the parcel.'

'That's all very well, but... How can I check up on you?'

'I won't be running away from this here spot.'

'Goose Farm? You live at Goose Farm?'

'I've nowhere else, see. I do the farm work.'

'Will you wait a minute while I talk to my colleagues?'

'You go ahead.'

The spokesman and two of the others huddle together beside the car, their soft black shoes already covered with mud and their heads of hair flattened by the drizzle.

At length they slosh across to be under the roof of the shed. One of them withdraws an outsize golden envelope from a flat leather document case.

'Mr Yockenthwaite, have you ever heard of the Once in a Lifetime Lottery?' he asked.

'Ar.'

'Have you got the ticket?'

'Ar.'

'Can you show it to me.'

'I can.'

5

'Please show me.'

Shadrach reached with difficulty into an undergarment, pulled out a small purse, opened the catch with a shaky hand and produced a ticket.

The spokesman glanced at it.

'That seems to be in order. Thank you. Now I have here a receipt, our evidence that you have received this envelope. Are you prepared to sign?'

'I don't mind.'

'You must understand that we'll be keeping a watchful eye on developments in the near future. We've decided to give you the benefit of the doubt. Should any irregularities come to light, the penalties would be severe.'

'Ar.'

'Where could we go for you to sign the receipt?'

'What's wrong out here?'

'You'll need a flat surface.'

Mr Yockenthwaite wiped with a sweep of his arm a level sheet of metal belonging to a piece of rusty farm machinery.

'That's too dirty,' the spokesman objects.

'It'll do.'

'Oh very well!'

The sheet of paper is laid on the metal. A pen is proffered. Shadrach Yockenthwaite slowly reads the writing on the receipt – or seems to.

A second dark-suited man mutters: 'We haven't got all day,' and a third says under his breath, 'Agricultural time!'

'I don't have my spectacles handy.'

The four men lose patience audibly. One says, 'Oh come on!' Another growls, 'You don't have to see to sign on the dotted line.' Yet another moans, 'What a mess – we could have done this by post!'

Shadrach speaks.

'Above board, is it?'

The visitors burst out laughing and jeering. The envelope is handed over. Shadrach opens it and extracts a large piece of paper. He glances at it and replaces it in the envelope.

The spokesman asks: 'Have you read it, sir?'

'I have.'

'No further comment?'

'Nar.'

'You can't have read it carefully.'

'I'll do that later.'

'You must have missed the point.'

'Don't you tell me my business! Where's that pen?'

The four men exchange glances and asides, expressive of amazement, disbelief, scorn and irritation.

Shadrach takes more time to sign his name.

He says: 'That all?'

'We think it's enough, sir, and more than enough. Thank you. Good day.'

They cross the yard, cursing the mud, and one of them says loudly: 'Talk of pearls before swine! Let's keep the bloody champagne for ourselves!' They clamber into the car, which moves silently to bump and stick in the puddles of the drive.

Shadrach hobbles towards the house, unlocks a door, enters, finds his spectacles on the kitchen table, puts them on his nose, takes off his sou'wester and crosses to the window, where he again opens the envelope. He holds in his hands an outsize cheque. He cannot understand the figures on the cheque, but gradually deciphers the writing: seventy-two-million four hundred and sixty-three thousand four hundred and eighty pounds only.

His face was made of cracked leather, his eyes were colourless and small, he had one or two yellow teeth, and as usual he had ten days' growth of beard. He was more than half a hermit, a miser, scared of authority, sixty-four years of age, waiting for his old age pension.

He reread the cheque repeatedly. At last he registered the fact that he had been given, won, somehow come into possession of, millions of pounds. He opened his mouth wide and uttered a loud noise between a scream, a shriek, a bellow, a roar. He then fell backwards, hitting his head on the floor. He had had a sort of seizure.

Shadrach Yockenthwaite was the scion of an old family. He was the son and grandson of peasants, and his wife had been a peasant, too. To the best of his own and general knowledge, his forefathers and close relations were all clodhoppers, sons and daughters of the soil, lumpkins, dunderheads, slaves of cows and pigs, employees of tight-fisted smallholders, and scraping a living in the mucky bottom of the social pile. Most of them had died young of agricultural mishaps, gored by bulls, chopped by porkers, mangled in machinery, poisoned by manure, not to mention overwork and exposure to the weather.

He was the third son of his father. The eldest, Tom, emigrated; the second, Arthur, disappeared; their sisters left home: Shadrach was meant to be the comfort of his parents. But his father was stamped on by a carthorse, and Shadrach aged twelve had to work for Mr Tyler of Goose Farm in order to feed himself and his mother. He worked for Farmer Tyler for fifty years, buried his mother, married, sired a son, buried his wife, was a lonely widower, and got Goose Farm for his pains. His bachelor employer left it to Shadrach to make up for having paid him starvation wages for half a century. It was not valuable, the hill soil was not worth cultivating and the buildings were rotting. Living in the farmhouse was almost as uncomfortable as sleeping on straw in a former stable. He sold an occasional acre in order to pay for essentials – he did not work the farm, he grew tomatoes and cabbages, picked his apples and blackberries, and went to bed early, feeling hungry. He was too stubborn to change his ways. He was too stubborn not to survive.

Shadrach Yockenthwaite came to on his kitchen floor. He did not recognise the paper in his hand. He readjusted his spectacles, reread the cheque and decided it was a fraud. He made tea and wondered who was pulling his leg. The world had always been cruel to Shadrach.

Later he dared to wonder if the cheque could

mean some of what it said in writing. He had bought a ticket in a sweepstake at The Queen's Head. He could remember it because he paid a pound for the ticket. He had been drunk – he would never have gambled away a pound sober.

He walked to the roadside pub about twice a year. He drank half pints of bitter morosely, talking to no one until he did his tipsy turn. His turn was to make a sort of speech to the assembled company. He would stand on shaky legs, brandish his half pint beer mug, and loudly slur out a repetitive rigmarole. 'I am Yockenthwaite of Goose Farm,' it began. 'Bow down to a Yockenthwaite born and bred. My family's good as yours, better and bigger. Believe me! Yocken means oxen, and a thwaite's a field – we've been in farming for ever and a day. Salt of the earth we are! Hurrah! Goo' night and goo'bye!' He would then collapse and be carried out, and eventually stagger home, along the road, up the cart-track, to his decaying homestead with its black metal weathervane toppling to the south.

He had found that ticket on the morning after and put it in his purse, which was not often opened. He now remembered filling in the other part of the ticket, and that it promised him the chance of winning big money. A man had said his pound would win him a Lottery Rollover, a Sweepstake on the Derby, a National Savings Once in a Lifetime offer, and the Canadian Golden Chance, all combining to pay out a record jackpot. He was convinced, convinced that he would win damn-all – he had never won anything. He mourned his expenditure of a pound. The cheque he was looking at was more than likely a mistake. He only believed bad news. But he was at least pleased to recall that he had ticked the 'privacy' box on the form.

Little by little he spotted holes in his pessimistic argument. Could the cheque be a practical joke or a con trick? Four complete strangers from nowhere would not dress in dark suits and hire a luxury saloon in order to deliver a phoney cheque to a Yockenthwaite on the breadline. Four confidence tricksters would not come to Goose Farm to get soaking wet and to muck up their fancy footwear for no discernible gain. The cheque, the paper written on, was kosher – Shadrach could be sure of that. What was written on it was the sticking point. Winnings of seventy-two millions were unheard of. By every law of averages the sum was incredible.

A few days fraught with interior controversy, soaring hopes, deep despair, passed slowly for Shadrach Yockenthwaite. One morning he had a good wash in water boiled on his electric stove, shaved with a not too rusty razor-blade, put on a cleaner shirt and buttoned it at the neck, donned a suit of Donegal tweed that had been worn by Farmer Tyler for many years, squeezed his swollen feet into shoes, and caught the bus into town at the bus-stop a mile or so from the bottom of his drive.

He had made an appointment with the manager of his bank, it had not been easy, the person he

11

spoke to asked if he was after another loan. The manager was late, he made Shadrach wait for twenty minutes before a secretary fetched him and ushered him in.

The Manager, Mr Burns, a small man with a bristling moustache, pointed to a chair on the other side of his desk, and began by saying: 'Your account is overdrawn, Mr Yockenthwaite.'

Shadrach cleared his throat phlegmatically.

'Are you on benefit, Mr Yockenthwaite? The government could help you in one way or another, no doubt.'

'I'm not begging, if that's on your mind.'

'I can't help thinking you're hard up.'

'You think what you like.'

'Oh well ... I don't have much time, Mr Yockenthwaite. Why did you want to see me?'

'You'll have time.'

'Excuse me?'

'Suppose a man had come into money?'

'Is that a question?'

'Could be.'

'Please repeat your question.'

'Aren't you in the money business?'

'What are you talking about?'

'I've got a fat cheque.'

'Mr Yockenthwaite, cheques are dealt with at the counter. If there were a large cheque, I'd ask to see it and require proof of its authenticity.'

'That's right.'

'Why did you make an appointment, sir?'

'What proofs?'

'Really, this is beside the point.'

'You tell me or you'll regret it.'

'What? Are you threatening me?'

'I'm saving you a red face.'

'What are you getting at?'

'You answer me.'

'Proofs – well, source of the payment, and identity of payee. I'm sorry, I must ask another question – are you feeling well?'

'Are you?'

'That'll do, Mr Yockenthwaite.'

'It won't, you know. You'll know soon, that is. Would you cash a cheque from another bank?'

'What bank?'

'A top one?'

'What do you mean by top? Why the secrecy, Mr Yockenthwaite? What's going on?'

'You'll see – it'll do you good.'

'But you haven't answered my question.'

'Nor have you answered mine.'

'Oh very well – yes, of course we'd accept a cheque from a respectable financial source for paying into a client's account.'

'No upper limit?'

'Mr Yockenthwaite, your account is two hundred and eighty six pounds in the red.'

'I could settle it.'

'Could you? May I ask when?'

'When I please.'

'Today?'

'If I was minded to.'

'Can I ask…?'

'That you can't, not yet, not while I'm thinking if you're to be trusted.'

13

'Mr Yockenthwaite, we're here to serve you to the best of our ability, as we always have.'

'Ta.'

Shadrach stood up.

'What are you doing, sir?'

'Saying bye-bye.'

'Have you no more to say in the business line?'

'Another day.'

Mr Burns also stood, and followed rather than escorted Shadrach out of the bank, shaking his head and grimacing at his colleagues.

The 'other day' occurred ten days later. Mr Burns received a telephone call – the staff at the bank had been persuaded to put Mr Yockenthwaite through to the manager.

'Want to see you private,' Shadrach stated. 'You come out here and I'll show you – and private, or else!'

'What are you playing at?'

'Could be your job – you'll lose it if you don't do as I say.'

'I will not be threatened, Mr Yockenthwaite – this is most irregular.'

'You come to Goose Farm round five o'clock, see?'

'I can't do that...'

'You'd better. I'll meet you at the bottom of my drive. Five o'clock, agreed!'

Mr Burns did not agree. But Shadrach had rung off, and Mr Burns discovered that Goose Farm had no telephone number. What did the 'or else' signify? Curiosity reinforced by fear caused him to motor out of town and draw up beside the unprepossessing figure standing on the verge of the Goose Farm cart-track. It was again a damp day. Shadrach wore his sou'wester, and the old sacks were over his shoulders. Mr Burns wound down the window of the car.

'What is it this time, Mr Yockenthwaite?' he demanded.

'Anybody know where you are?'

'Oh for goodness' sake!'

'Look here then,' said Shadrach. He produced the golden envelope from within his layers of clothing, extracted the cheque, and, sheltering it from the damp air, held it for a few seconds within sight of Mr Burns.

Exclamations ensued.

'What's this? ... What have you got there? ... What's it say? ... Oh dear! ... Mercy me! ... Oh heavens! ... Mr Yockenthwaite!'

Shadrach replaced the cheque in the envelope, stowed it away, peered at Mr Burns from under the brim of his sou'wester, grinned at him showing a yellow tooth, and said in a menacing tone: 'If you gab you won't see it no more.'

'Oh, I promise you – please tell me – what am I to do?'

'I'm thinking I'll have an account with a cheque book, but private – London maybe, not hereabouts.'

'Would you like to visit our Head Office in London, Mr Yockenthwaite? I could arrange that.'

'Could you now?'

'Would you like me to open the account at my branch, sir?'

'I won't have people knocking on my door. It'll be public if your branch has it. A banker from London could come and sign for the cheque.'

'Come to Goose Farm?'

'What's wrong with that?'

'Well, I'm sure Head Office would be willing to oblige you.'

'I shouldn't wonder. I'll be needing a word of advice, too.'

'We have a department of qualified advisers who would be pleased to offer their expertise.'

'Department don't sound right – I don't want to please no one.'

'Quite so, sir.'

'You get me a best banker with some names and addresses in his head.'

'Whose names, Mr Yockenthwaite?'

'International.'

'Would you not wish to keep all your money in England?'

'I haven't said nothing. We'll see. A banker with no wagging tongue – you find him – and if he's not satisfactory I'll kick him out.'

'I understand your feelings, sir. I'll submit an urgent request for a top officer of the bank to meet you at your convenience.'

'You'll be my witness, and I'll want a recording of what's said and done.'

'Very good, sir. Could I trouble you for another sight of the cheque? I'll be needing details.'

'I don't want it getting wet...'

'Of course, sir. I should explain that we will have to check that the money exists and is available. We always have to study the paper-work.'

'Don't you go charging me interest on my overdraft meanwhile!'

Mr Burns sniggered sycophantically, and said: 'No, no, sir, nothing like that – we are in debt to you for offering us the business in hand. Would you like me to drive you to your home, Mr Yockenthwaite?'

'No fear – you'll be running up costs if I'm not careful.'

Shadrach walked uphill with unwonted briskness. He was no longer the man he had been for half a century. He was like one of those seeds that hide underground for decades and unexpectedly decide to flower. Seventy-two million could afford a transformation scene. The threadbare curmudgeon, the thick yokel, uncom-municative and bitter, all was undergoing a sea change. He had acquired confidence. He had made the quantum leap into a new world, if not a better one. He, who had been bossed about by other people, his father who died, his mother who spent his money, his wife who got herself with child, and his oppressive employer, Farmer Tyler – he was the master now.

Decision One was to secrete his wealth. Two was to steer clear of open hands. Three was to keep out of the limelight. Four was to give nothing to his son, Robert, and so it went on. Philanthropy was absent from his plans.

The flower that sprouted from the seed called Shadrach was not pretty. It was more carnivorous than pretty. Gold was a blunt instrument in his narrowed eyes rather than a chance to give presents. Wealth cleared his brain, which had been fogged up by petty concerns such as where the next meal was coming from and the slights and injustice he was suffering. Now he could have his revenge. He was not happy. He did not know what happiness was. But at least he had something to look forward to, other than kicks in his remaining teeth. He would count his money. He had real money, millions of it to count, millions that were his and no one else's, millions never to be shared. He had won the right to work out how to be a multimillionaire.

Manna was falling from heaven into the pocket of Shadrach Yockenthwaite – he had had a birthday and been into town to collect his first week's pension. He was not religious in spite of having had his knuckles rapped in Bible Class in the dark age of his childhood. He had no reason to love God, on the contrary; but his name was bibilical, and after all his faith in envy and avarice had been rewarded.

His mind seemed to him to be making up for the time he had wasted in stupidity, and his body was shedding lethargy as if it had been a superfluous skin. But the process cut both ways. He was at once set free and imprisoned. He was richer than he had ever dared to dream of being, and worse off than he had ever imagined he could be.

Having always wanted to get his hands on other people's money, he now suspected the whole world was wanting to get their hands on his. He was assailed by frightening questions and answers, first, what to do with his wealth, secondly how to guard and protect it, and then that it could be stolen, he could awake from the dream of his millions to discover he was destitute. Behind his locked doors, he stared suspiciously through closed windows, and waited and worried. In his glum opinion an extraordinarily good experience began to look not much better than the bad one.

He had not yet cashed his cheque. He had taken no decision, he had been as negative as he had been when he was poor. He had shown the banker from London and Mr Burns the door, the exit from Goose Farm. He had resented the banker's disappointing, patronising and proprietary attitude, withstood his reproaches, and rejected Mr Burns' plea for common sense to prevail. Shadrach commandeered the tape of their interview and told them to go to hell.

Then somebody must have leaked or sneaked that he had money coming out of his ears. In the old days, Goose Farm had received only bills by post. Now the postman was delivering appeals. The charities had his name and address, the do-gooders were nagging him, the lunatic fringe threatened to take his money by force if persuasion failed, the Africans wanted him to save them from themselves, and the Inland Revenue was getting him down with their brown envelopes.

'Robbers,' he called them. 'Robbers and thieves!'

He loaded Mr Tyler's rook rifle and brought indoors a length of lead piping. He was ready to fight off all intruders, old as he was. At the same time he concluded that he would have to seek salvation in the modern manner. Eventually he donned Mr Tyler's suit again and caught a bus to London.

He had never been there before. He booked a room in a B&B near the terminus. He skulked about, ate sandwiches, drank tea from automats, shunned pubs where he might consume too many half pints and increase the dangers he was incessantly feeling he was in. He expected to be mugged at least. He might be tortured until he wrote some criminal a cheque for seventy-two million. He met nobody's eyes and wore his sou'wester even when the sun shone – to hide under, although it attracted attention. He moved from one B&B to another every few days to cover his tracks. He was miserable but used to that; he was also content to suffer for the sake of his money.

He was not idle. After seeking help in Information Offices and the Yellow Pages, he decided on impulse, perhaps because he was so tired, to take a frightful risk. He decided to ring the doorbell of a certain Harold Webber, Accountancy and Financial Services. Mr Webber's entry in the Yellow Pages was smaller and more modest than others, and his office had the attraction for Shadrach of being located in Shepherds Market. He braved the stares of West

End people and found a door with Harold Webber's name on it. He rang and climbed to the fourth floor of an old building with no lift. A stolid man with a dark skin and a polite smile admitted him. The room had a desk, hard chairs, computers and tall metal files.

Shadrach sat on a hard chair and said: 'I'm wanting service.'

He did not expect to get it. He was not sure he would like to be served by the man who had let him in. He braced himself for rudeness and rejection.

'That's my business,' the man replied.

Shadrach took off his sou'wester.

'I've money to invest,' he said.

'What sort of sum would that be, little or large?'

'Not little.'

'One hundred pounds or a million?'

'More than that.'

'Much more?'

'Ar.'

'How do you wish to invest it?'

'Out of reach.'

'We'd have to trust each other before I could take responsibility for your money.'

'My money's in cash, and I'll be wanting it kept that way, and you bound hand and foot by contracts.'

'A colleague of mine works in a branch of a private Austrian-Swiss bank. Would it be worth his while to join us?'

'Ar.'

21

'Tomorrow morning?'

'Ar.'

'Eleven-thirty?'

'Ar.'

'I don't know your name, sir, or where you live. You can choose to attend our meeting tomorrow or not to attend. I would like you to know that I'm a chartered accountant, work alone, my fees are at the low end of the scale of accountants' charges, but my clients pay me a living wage. I was not born and bred in England, I would claim to be a patriotic Englishman in all other respects – my wife and my children are English.'

'Ta,' Shadrach said.

He returned on the following day, but brought his tape recorder along – it was switched on before the meeting began.

Mr Webber introduced Mr Elsen of the Maria Theresa Bank to Mr Yockenthwaite of Goose Farm. In due course the cheque drawn in favour of Mr S. Yockenwhwaite was produced and shown round. The two professionals did not make too much fuss about it, which reassured Shadrach. He was asked what he had meant by saying he wished the money to be 'out of reach'.

'Don't want the government to get it and waste it, nor crooks pretending to be family. It's for me, see.'

They asked his age, and chattered together in terms he did not understand.

Harold Webber gave their advice.

'You are not liable for tax on winnings such

as yours, and you're free to invest your money offshore. We suggest that you purchase non-interest-bearing deposits in so-called tax havens, Switzerland with its numbered accounts, for example, and Monaco and the Cayman Islands. These investments could be repayable after a year or after longer periods. We can produce a list and a schedule for your inspection. By following our advice your capital would be as safe as possible, you could have ample money available at all times, either because an investment has matured or you are borrowing against one that's about to mature, and you will have no income that might attract the taxman. If or when you feel able to agree our plan, you could open an account with Mr Elsen's bank and in principle and in writing instruct myself and Mr Elsen to buy the securities. Contracts would be issued for each purchase, and you would instruct us to charge our costs and fees. The signing ceremonies could take place either in Mr Elsen's bank with additional witnesses, or here in my office with or without the presence of a solicitor for oaths.'

Shadrach told them to get on with it. In twenty-four hours, back in Mr Webber's office, he received the paraphernalia of a new customer of the Maria Theresa Bank, and signed his name until his hand ached. Three days later, in the same place, he was signing cheques for sums of money that made his head spin, and feeling quite sick when he had to part with the golden piece of paper that was worth seventy-two million.

He returned to Goose Farm. He had another

financial task to perform: he was discovering that the work of a multimillionaire is never done. There had been some discussion with Messrs Webber and Elsen of how much money Mr Yockenthwaite would wish to retain to cover his expenses until the first 'bond' repaid its several millions. Shadrach said that the sixty-three thousand four hundred and eighty pounds would suffice. The others were surprised to hear it. They ventured to point out tactfully that at his age, and because he had no known heirs, he might consider spending more of his great fortune. 'Nar,' he said. He meant that he would spend a lot less than tens of thousands. He was then advised to pay the sum in question into an account at his local bank – it would be more practical than expecting an Austrian-Swiss investment bank to pay for his groceries.

Shadrach took the bus into Teasham. He was hoping to pay his cheque into his account at the counter, as once advised to do by the manager. He did not want to see Mr Burns; but Mr Burns saw him. And Mr Burns invited him forcibly into his private office.

What had become of the rest of Mr Yockenthwaite's money, he wished to know.

'Gone,' Shadrach replied.

'Gone where?'

'West or east,' said Shadrach with a rare touch of humour.

'What do you mean, sir?'

'Lost.'

'Have you lost it gambling?'

'You could say so.'

'What a shame, Mr Yockenthwaite. This bank and its officers made great efforts to assist you to safeguard all that money.'

'That's a fact.'

'Will you be making a will, Mr Yockenthwaite?'

'What's that?'

'A will and testament is a guide for the solicitor who manages your estate in the event of your death. If you should need a solicitor to advise you, may I recommend Mr Chimbley of Chimbley Chimbley and Davis, Mr Chimbley Junior? Mr Chimbley's office is just across the way and I can recommend the firm warmly.'

'Not a lawyer?'

'Well, yes, but Mr Chimbley Senior is retired now, and young Mr Chimbley's a helpful individual. Shall I give you his calling card?'

'Up to you.'

'Thank you, sir. I hope we'll be seeing you often in the branch.'

'Ta-ta.'

Shadrach returned to Goose Farm. He behaved as before. He could not break his habits. The main change was that he considered his health, ate a piece of meat when it was marked down at the butcher's, and brought better stuff at the supermarket.

Otherwise, he spent his time doing sums on scraps of paper, which he tore into shreds and tossed into the fireplace in the sitting-room.

The fireplace gave him an idea. He had not yet found a good hiding place for his bundle of papers relating to the transactions in London. The list of his portfolio of investments, the contract notes, and letters from Harold Webber and Mr Elsen had been moved from behind the downstairs lav to a shed in the yard, into a tin buried in the garden, and back indoors, pushed into the toes of a pair of old wellies. The grate in the fireplace was cast iron, but the chimney was built before iron grates were mass-produced. Long ago Farmer Tyler had shown Shadrach that a recess in the brickwork was accessible by reaching up right-handed. Papers secreted there would never be found. Shadrach wrapped his in a crumpled plastic bag and stowed them in the recess, where bread had once been made.

Time passed. The rook rifle and the lead pipe were still kept in handy positions. But Shadrach was less afraid of being visited by criminals. He had possessions he could afford to hand over to burglars, if need be. Let them ransack his home, they would find nothing of value! Let them twist his arm, his millions were elsewhere and inaccessible.

One evening he walked to The Queen's Head. He thought he was safe to do so, and he fancied a drink, he felt he deserved one, he argued that he could afford one, and he would celebrate both his luck and its concealment.

He sat in his rags in a corner of the pub with his half pint of bitter beer. He enjoyed the thought that he was richer than anyone else there. He was richer than all of them put together. He went back to the bar, ordered another half pint, produced his purse, paid in small change and returned to his seat. After several refills he had only spoken three or four words, 'Evening ... Usual ... Ta ... Same again!'

He stood up as if to approach the bar for more beer and began to shout and gesticulate. Older customers knew his ways, younger ones who had never seen a Shadrach performance were amused, but the girls screamed.

'Yockenthwaites rule the world,' he seemed to be saying between chesty coughs. 'We're silver and gold. We are! I could buy this pub twice over. Yockenthwaites wherever you are, God bless! Yockenthwaites for ever! Goo'bye!'

He tried to turn round but fell over backwards, spraying beer and hitting his head on a table. When the landlord and volunteers tried to pick him up, he kicked out and cursed them. He struggled to his feet, stumbled out of the pub and along the road, collapsed in his drive, and eventually reached base.

Afterwards he was not himself: he often wondered who he was. His recent intermittent feelings that he was financially secure, and life might be worth living for a change, were irrecoverable. Anxiety possessed him. His chronic fear because he had been poor was nothing compared with his fear because he was rich and might cease to be at any moment. The countries he had invested in could go bust or disappear off the map. The Maria Theresa Bank could be a front for conmen and gangsters. What reason had he had to entrust his wealth to Harold

Webber and Mr Elsen? It had been madness! He saw seventy-two million gurgling down the drain. All that was left was paper, bits of paper, but legal, they were as good as his money or nearly, they were, they had been signed and sealed. He would check again and get the better of those rascals in London.

Where were his papers?

He searched for them. He remembered having hidden letters and contract notes where a burglar would never find them: but where? He searched for days. He took the shreds of paper out of the grate in the sitting room, matched one with another, and did not find what he was looking for. He began to feel sick without it. He could not eat or sleep. Charities' appeals for his money littered the sitting-room floor: they were after his money, they seemed to say he had millions, but could they prove it, and, if not, would the charities be charitable to him? He tore them up, one at a time, shaking them, shaking the envelopes, and piled them on top of the shreds already in the grate. One day he resolved to tidy the sitting-room, destroy all the misleading stuff in there, and to look again in the other rooms of Goose Farm. There was a box of matches on the mantelshelf. He lit a match and held it near the shreds, and then he heard himself moaning and squeaking as the papers burst into flames.

Second Chapter of Nine

A young man was boarding an intercontinental flight from Australia to Britain via Singapore and Dubai. His full head of blond hair was shoulder length. He was clean-shaven, suntanned, blue-eyed, a big boy, upstanding, but already fleshy and with the beginnings of a beer belly. He wore a T-shirt, jeans with holes at knee level, and scuffed trainers. The message on the T-shirt was 'Aussies 10 Poms 0', and he had a tattoo of the Australian flag on his right upper arm. His luggage was a rucksack. He cracked old jokes with airline staff and laughed at them loudly. His name was Wayne Yockenthwaite.

His obvious excitement was due to several causes. He had received a letter from England, from a man called Chimbley, a solicitor in a firm called Chimbley Chimbley and Davis of Teasham in Gloucestershire, informing him that if he would report to the solicitor's office at his earliest convenience, he would receive news greatly to his advantage. The letter was a bit of a thrill, and another bit was the money enclosed for a first class air ticket in a reputable airline to Heathrow, London. Moreover, it would be his first flight. He was also bubbling over because he had pulled a fast one. He had bought an economy class ticket with the first class money and chosen to fly with a third-rate company, Magic Carpet Airborne. There were not many people on his flight, he had shown his letter from Mr Chimbley to the airport people, said he would always fly with Magic Carpet if they treated him right, and been upgraded to a seat in business class, the best available.

The business class passengers boarded first. There were only four of them, an elderly couple, a middle-aged lady and the young man. They were greeted at the door of the aeroplane by a steward in a blue uniform and a stewardess with dark hair and bright eyes that seemed to glitter. Their hand luggage was carried by the pair of cabin staff and they were ushered up the staircase and into the business class compartment. It had twenty seats, a low ceiling, and musak.

The steward accompanied the three older passengers to seats near the front, a double for the couple on the left of the aisle, one for the lady two rows back on the right. The stewardess introduced herself to the last passenger.

'I'm Milly, sir, and I'll be looking after you on this flight.'

'Hi, Milly. I'm Wayne. Pleased to meet you, I'm sure,' he replied.

'Where would you like to sit, sir?'

'You tell me, Milly – what's my seat number?'

'That won't apply, sir – I only have the four passengers this time round – you can sit where you please.'

'What about a back seat, Milly – I always like a back seat at the movies.'

She smiled, she knew what he was talking about, but answered respectfully: 'You can suit yourself, sir.'

He extended his hand and said: 'You call me Wayne, Milly – let's shake on it!' He squeezed her hand hard. 'Do we get any entertainment, Milly?'

'Two films are shown.'

'They'd better be long ones. Maybe we'll have a chat, Milly?'

'I have my duties to attend to, but you never know.'

'Wouldn't you like to hear my life story?'

'I've heard some of those.'

'I should think you have, Milly.'

The steward arrived on the scene.

'Is Milly taking care of you, sir?'

'I should say so!'

'She's in charge here.'

'Too true!'

'But you can call me by pressing the buzzer.'

'What's the name, mate, if I may ask – Christian name?'

'George, sir.'

'I'm Wayne, you're George – okay? Let's shake!'

They shook hands, laughing, and George said bye-bye to Wayne.

Milly asked: 'Would you like me to stow your hand luggage in the locker?'

'I certainly would, Milly.'

'Do you want to take out a jumper or a jacket – it can be chilly on the flight?'

'Heck, no – I've got my thermostat to keep me warm.'

'Very well.'

She reached up to open the locker, and reached up again to stow the rucksack, thus twice adopting the pose that shows off the female form to the best advantage.

Wayne murmured under his breath, having watched her, 'Gee whiz!' He laughed, she laughed, their flirting was conspiratorial, and she excused herself to talk to her three other customers.

After take-off a meal was served. Wayne and Milly became more friendly while she served it, and when it was all done, and the first of the two films was showing, they had their chat. She sat in the free seat next to Wayne's and asked him questions.

'Don't you want to watch the film, Wayne?'

He did not – it was about a baby – he would puke if he saw any more of it.

'Well – how come a young bloke like you can afford to travel business?'

'Nothing but the best, Milly,' he fibbed. 'What the hell! I think I've had a little windfall.'

'Do you mean you're rich, Wayne?'

'Yes – and no – could be.'

'You've got holes in your jeans.'

'Like them that way! I'm telling you, my trousers may look poor but my legs are pure gold underneath.'

'I might check up on them. Seriously, how come you're rich?'

He hesitated, but did not expect ever to see her again, and was tempted to confide in her.

'I'm a pom, Milly – English by birth, Aussie by nature – and brought up in Harvestide, at the back of Bourke – that's in the outback, see? My pa was a skint farmer, but my granpa had the money – and he's left some of it to me.'

'How much?'

'That'd be telling.'

'Go on, Wayne!'

'Could be a brick.'

'What's that?'

'A cool million, I'm guessing.'

'You're a lucky boy.'

'I am that.'

'What about your parents?'

'Pa's dead – he missed out by a whisker – so I get the dosh.'

'And your mother?'

'She's joined him. She was terminal.'

'Poor her! So you're flying off to England to collect your money?'

'That's about the size of it. There's a farmhouse too. My granpa was a so-and-so, but he's done me a good turn, he has, no sweat.'

'Where's the house?'

'In the West Country.'

'I like that part of the world. I might look you up there.'

'Might you just?'

'Thanks for the invitation, Wayne.'

He laughed off her sarcasm.

She asked: 'But how did your grandfather have all this money?'

'We don't rightly know – could have robbed

a bank – who cares? – the money's good – my first port of call's a solicitor's office down that way, in a town name of Teabag.'

They had a giggle.

'What are you going to spend a million pounds on?' she asked.

'Wine and women maybe.'

'No wife?'

'Not one – no babies either, Milly.'

'You'll have to watch your back, won't you?'

'See if you can get past me!'

'You're very suspicious. You lead women on when you say you're cleverer than they are. What makes you so sure of yourself?'

'We were sharp in Harvestide, we were ahead of the game.'

'Fancy that! What's your surname, Wayne?'

'That's a spot of bother – it's English – I'll be paying to change it.'

'Tell me before you do.'

'Oh well – okay – Yockenthwaite.'

She laughed at it, at him, and he joined in. Then she had duties; she gave him more magazines to look at; and eventually they landed at Singapore.

Night was falling when they left on the second leg of their journey. Milly served dinner – no one else had swelled the numbers in business class – and then put on another film. It was soft porn, and in places not exactly soft. Milly had cleared the dinner and settled down her other customers for the night. She joined Wayne who was watching the film wide-eyed.

'Strewth, Milly,' he said to her, 'you'd have to go far in Australia to find a film like this one!'

'Do you like it?'

'I certainly do.'

'Would you like to be in bed with that girl, Wayne?'

'I wouldn't say no.'

'Would you like to be doing those things?'

'You're talking broad now, Milly.'

'Are you getting excited?'

'Good grief, Milly!'

'Wayne, have you ever heard of the Mile High Club?'

'Can't say I have. One of those snobby clubs, is it?'

'Not really – I could make you a member.'

'That's good of you, Milly. Can't be too snobby then. Where does it hang out?'

'It's worldwide.'

'No! And what do you get for your money?'

'I'll show you, if you wait a minute.'

'Are you getting me a brochure?'

'You could put it that way.'

The minute passed. She returned and said something in his ear about stripping for action. She then initiated him into The Mile High Club expertly, undoing his trousers, raising her skirt out of the line of fire, lowering herself into his lap, hushing him and stifling her own grunts and groans. He was pleasantly surprised to be a Member, and both he and she had time to make themselves look respectable before they landed in Dubai.

Later, between Dubai and London, daylight and sunshine flooded into the business class, and George the steward put in appearances. The other passengers, walking to and from the toilet, also inhibited private transactions between Wayne and Milly. He helped her with his rucksack and she repaid him with a licentious kiss; but when he left the aeroplane she stood by George and bade him goodbye with only the hint of a wink.

Wayne Yockenthwaite continued his journey to the West Country by hitch-hikes and Shanks' pony – he had very little cash in his purse and was loath to spend it, his possible inheritance notwithstanding. Eventually he rang the doorbell of a picturesque old townhouse in a cobbled yard. Affixed to the door was a worn yet brightly polished brass plate bearing the legend, Chimbley Chimbley and Davis, Solicitors. He was admitted by a grey-haired man in a black three-piece suit, who looked askance at the T-shirt etc, asked for the name and business of the caller, carefully read the letter he was shown, admitted Wayne and showed him into a dark and cheerless waiting-room.

A quarter of an hour elapsed.

Another man in a three-piece suit entered the waiting-room. He was neither old nor young, he was dignified, polite and professional.

'Good afternoon, Mr Yockenthwaite,' he said. 'My name is Chimbley, I'm Mr Morgan Chimbley.'

They shook hands.

'Begging your pardon, mister, I can't stick that name of mine,' Wayne said. 'Could we cut the cackle? I'm Wayne.'

'As you please sir.'

'What'll I call you? Would you be okay with Morgan?'

'Mr Chimbley would be preferable.'

'That so? Well – I'm not fussy when a man's going to hand over money – I hope!'

'Shall we adjourn to my room?'

It was dark there, too. Black tin boxes with names in white painted on them were stacked one on top of another against the walls. The two men sat on either side of an antique kneehole desk.

'You received the advance of funds that I sent you, Wayne?'

'Sure did – came in handy.'

'I would like to extend condolences for the loss of your parents.'

'Your first letter tipped Pa over the edge – he'd been on his uppers, see?'

'I'm sorry.'

'To be truthful, Mr Chimbley, can't say I am – human nature, mate.'

'No doubt you'd wish to know how your grandfather passed over?'

'I'd like to know where he got his bread.'

'He won the money in some international lottery. The total sum is extremely large, we understand, but where it is, what has happened to it, what your grandfather did with it, and where it will end up, are unknown factors. I believe, therefore, that we should concentrate on the available evidence. The organisation that promoted the lottery has disappeared off the face of the earth. Anyway, your grandfather was found on the floor of the sitting-room of Goose Farm – his house, which will be yours, Wayne. He seems to have been burning papers in the grate – the room was full of charred pieces of paper. His right hand was burnt – the police thought he might have reached into the flames, perhaps to rescue a particular piece of paper. But that's speculation. He died of a heart attack. I regret to say he wasn't found for a month.'

'Did you find him, Mr Chimbley?'

'It was the postman, whose suspicions were aroused by the squeaks of rodents in the sitting-room.'

'Rats, you mean?'

'I'm afraid so.'

'Hard lines, granpappy!'

'I did not know Mr Shadrach Yockenthwaite personally. He died alone, and he left some questions unanswered. The inheritance will now pass to his next of kin. I therefore asked you to submit to a DNA test, when I had discovered that your late father, Mr Shadrach's son, had expired.'

'No will?'

'No, not to the best of our knowledge.'

'Pardon me, Mr C, but that being so how did you get in on the act?'

'Through your grandfather's bank here, the National Westminster. The manager, Mr Burns,

and a gentleman from the Head Office of the
bank in London, Mr Macnaughton, had dealings
with your grandfather over his winnings. They
gave him advice. They instructed me to act on
behalf of your grandfather and his estate, and I
hope that meets with your approval.'

'I pay your bill, Mr Chimbley?'

'That is so – we will be submitting our note
of fee when the estate is wound up.'

'Do I need a lawyer for that stuff? I'm ready
to cough up for services rendered, but I'm not
a pom.'

'Mr Yockenthwaite was an independent-minded
man. He was eccentric, if I may say so. He was
reputed to be reluctant to spend money, and my
guess is that he was not keen to share his fortune
with the government.'

'I'm right behind him there.'

'Yes – well – I was instructed, and am in a
position to tell you it has taken me many moons
to be able to summon you from Australia. The
problems were, first, no paperwork to be found,
no contracts, nothing; secondly, your share of
your inheritance only came to light when it
arrived at the NatWest from a private bank in
the Cayman Islands; thirdly, via the Cayman
Islands and an obscure Swiss bank we traced a
Mr Webber, a financial adviser, but he was
suffering from dementia in North Yorkshire, and
could only tell us Mr Yockenthwaite's treasure
was well hidden; fourthly, finally, because of the
sequence of events, we have had to fight many
battles with the Inland Revenue, the tax gatherers.'

'Hidden, was it? What next, Mr C?'

'Obtaining probate – that is, clearance by the authorities was the difficulty. They wanted to tax the money, but couldn't find it, which was no doubt the object of your grandfather's financial arrangements.'

'I'm biting my nails, Mr Chimbley.'

'I'm sorry to have tested your patience as ours has been tested. You inherit five million pounds as well as Goose Farm.'

'Whoa ... Phew ... My word ... Turn on the fan, man! Well, I'll be ... Five million – I've been saying one for a joke – I expected a couple of hundred. Five million pounds – that's sterling, ain't it? – you've made me happy, Mr Chimbley.'

'The money is deposited in the bank, and I can introduce you to the manager, Mr Burns, when we've finished here.'

'I'll be glad to get my hot hands on it, I can promise you that, mister.'

'Your grandfather's account at the bank had a closing balance, a tidy sum, sixty-three odd thousands, which you also inherit.'

'Good old granpa! Five million!'

'The next thing on the agenda is subtractions, I regret to say.'

'Did I hear right?'

'You have tax to pay.'

'I thought you'd whacked the taxman?'

'The Inland Revenue couldn't tax your grandfather's winnings, they're not liable, but could collect death duty on the money you've inherited.'

'I'm not paying.'

'In that case you'll go to prison.'

'How much?'

'Forty per cent'

'That's for poms, they let their pockets be picked – I'm an Aussie – nobody takes good money off us.'

'Two million is owed to the government of this country.'

'You're joking, mate!'

'I never joke in business hours.'

'I'll ship out to Oz with the money.'

'There's an extradition treaty between England and Oz, you'll be brought back to pay the two million and probably another million in fines.'

'What would paying leave me with?'

'You want to know how much you'll have after deductions?'

'Yes, sir – straight between the eyes!'

'Our fee amounts to getting on for two hundred and fifty thousand pounds.'

'That's a joke! What are you talking about?'

'The administration of your grandfather's estate, and arriving at the point at which I can unite you with your inheritance, have taken us innumerable hours of work, including travel to London, Switzerland, the Cayman Islands in the Caribbean, and back to Switzerland on two occasions, and our legitimate fee for the work I am qualified to do would probably cost twice the sum I have mentioned if I were to charge the full amount. For you, Wayne, because I hope for work in the future in connection with your grandfather's estate, our fee will be reduced.'

'Reduced – oh heck! Mr Chimbley, you've kept me gossiping here and you must be paying your clock to tick. You're not taking me to see Mr Burns, I'll go alone, thanks a bunch! And I'll find my way to Goose Farm! You poms are hot as well as wet, I will say that for you.'

'Please remember that your grandfather's leading the dance.'

'Some dance! I'll be getting out of here chop-chop.'

'Shall I inform you in a letter of your debt owing to the Inland Revenue and how to pay it?'

'You do as you please, sir.'

'In a day or two you will receive at Goose Farm our note of fee, which will include VAT at nearly eighteen per cent.'

'Stone the crows! VAT, what's that?'

'Another government tax – you will have to pay both death duty and value added tax – by law, Wayne. You have come to live in a civilised country where the government confiscates everybody's money.'

'Not mine, cocky!'

'A last word, sir – I regret having to tell you the government gets its money by hook or crook, and that my firm sues without delay for unpaid invoices and claims damages on top of the money owed to us.'

'Let's have the keys to my hidey-hole!'

Wayne Yockenthwaite was a cheery boyo, but underneath he had a big grudge against the world. It was in his genes, he was born with it, and he saw injustice everywhere, not least since the two letters from Chimbley, Chimbley and Davis had arrived at the run-down smallholding where the family eked out an aimless existence. Joy was immediately followed by sorrow, or at least shock, when Wayne's father dropped dead; and then his mother was carted off to hospital en route to the morgue.

But after Wayne returned the legal letter together with a note to say his father and mother had both passed over, he himself received a similar summons. He was pleased, almost happy, which was a new experience. He knew money was on the menu and membership of the MHC was icing on the cake. The minutes when he was the possessor of five whole millions, untaxed, not nibbled into by vermin, he was happier than happy, he was ecstatic. The rest was disappointment and dirty work.

Goose Farm was no exception to his gloomy rule. It was a ruin. He walked up the drive. Brambles almost met in the middle, trees had taken over, stagnant water filled pools that once had been puddles. He saw the buildings at the top, and exclaimed inwardly: 'Where's the effing farm?' Roofs had fallen in, slates, joists, bricks were missing, even the rusty old machines were falling apart. The 'farmhouse' was almost lost under ivy and behind bay trees. The interior had obviously been home to bats as well as rats, pigeons, death-watch beetles and other insects, they had devoured the floorboards and most of the staircase. The only furniture was a plank of wood on bricks and upstairs the skeleton of an iron bedstead.

Wayne ate food he had bought in Teasham and looked on the dark side. Goose Farm was not so different from Harvestide: he would have to patch it up, he was back to patching up until kingdom come. He kicked out live rats, he chucked out dead pigeons. He spent a very few pounds on basic supplies, an axe and a saw, candles, old newspapers with which to block broken windowpanes, and a third-hand bicycle. He rendered the house habitable, not clean, not comfortable, but less unhealthy. He hacked down trees and burned the logs in the grate in the sitting-room. He slept on some musty hay he had found in the former stable. His jeans were more torn and his T-shirt was a rag; but what the hell, as he would have told his mates in Oz.

Instead of changing his clothes he changed his spots. He had said, he had believed he never would or could, but he did. He was not going back to Australia – those mates of his would pluck him in record time. No, he was a changed man, a rich man, and he was staying put and as close to his money as possible. He bicycled into Teasham, made a beeline for the office of Mr Burns, took charge of his inheritance, signed on dotted lines, opened accounts, obtained cheque books, and withdrew two hundred pounds in five-pound notes. He put the rest of his money in a reserve account paying a decent rate of interest. He then bought a children's calculator,

44

bicycled home, and worked out that after all disbursements he would be left with precisely two million three hundred and forty-four pounds and ninety pence.

It was not so good as it had been. Wayne Yockenthaite had a few nightmares in which his money had vanished and he was again scratching the dry earth in the outback. Three months had passed, and he took a perverse pride in demonstrating that he had managed to keep alive on the two hundred pounds.

His first visitor arrived one summer afternoon. It was a sheila in his lingo, and her name was Milly. She looked okay from a distance, in her neat clothes in the sunshine, but at closer quarters she was older than he remembered; and being hot and breathless after walking uphill did not so improve her appearance that he was pleased to see her. He went through the motions of hospitality.

'Hi, Milly,' he shouted at her.

'Aren't I clever to have tracked you to your lair?' she responded.

He noticed the capacious bag she was carrying, an overnight bag with no space to spare, and answered warily: 'Good of you to come to call.'

She laughed at his hint and wondered if she could have a glass of water. He said he would bring her out a cup. She laughed again and perched on a plank seat he had rigged up in the garden of Goose Farm – in fact it could hardly be called a garden, it was more like undergrowth. He went into the house, washed out one of the two teacups he had found in a cupboard, and made up his mind to get rid of Milly pdq – she was wanting something out of him, no question.

'Funny old place you've got here, Wayne,' she remarked, looking askance at the cup but refraining from sarcasm. 'And talking of funny old things, don't I recognise those shreds of trousers?'

'Correct there, Milly! I'll have to get another pair one of these days. How've you been, and where are you heading?'

She mumbled something about a friend in Glastonbury, and referred to a tour of the premises: 'Aren't you going to show me round your home?'

He had to say yes. Indoors they got a bit friendly. She reached out a hand for him to take and help her up the rickety stairs. And she laughed at the pile of hay in the front bedroom and called him a wild creature – or was he a koala bear? Then she asked to use the bathroom, unclean though it was. When she rejoined him she was more than friendly. She reminded him of the MHC, and put her hand through one of the holes in his jeans. They were both ready for everything, and the hay served another purpose. Afterwards, there was billing and cooing, and he said she could stay the night and, even more contrarily, let her have six five-pound notes to spend on food for a nice dinner and a taxi to the shops. She must have had more money of her own than she had revealed, for she brought back a cold roast chicken, vegetables, fruit, two bottles of wine, bacon and eggs, eating irons, and an outsize futon and coverlet. They ate well, made love, slept in between times on the futon, and breakfasted well. Then she told him she was pregnant.

He was scared, he was negative, he was bloody-minded: no babies, not one, no blackmail, no financial assistance, not a penny, and, he said, he was not playing her game nor was he having his tail twisted by any damn woman.

He was wrong. He ate his words and swallowed his principles. He was bribed physically and brainwashed by smiles, frowns, tears, reproaches and nagging, by bullying, threats of suicide and murder, and by having been knocked senseless by long days and disturbed nights. She knew what she wanted, had wanted from the moment she had caught the sweet smell of Wayne's money. Her wants were a gold ring on her finger, a name for their child, and a marriage settlement of five hundred thousand pounds. He married her, paid the blood money, and a daughter was duly borne, Diane Yockenthwaite. Meanwhile Wayne half-wished he was unrelated to old Shadrach. After six months of matrimonial disharmony Milly walked off the premises, abandoning husband and child, and sued for divorce – Mr Chimbley sent him a copy of the letter received from her London solicitor.

Wayne wheeled Diane in her pram into Teasham and the offices of Chimbley Chimbley and Davis.

Mr Morgan Chimbley's response to Wayne's tribulations was practical and prompt. The hypothetical father and the child must undergo

47

DNA tests; if Diane was not his child he must disown her. He must insert a notice in *The Times* to announce that he would not pay any bills his wife might run up. The divorce would be costly because of the unjust laws passed by politicians, he would probably have to give his wife half of all he possessed, including half of Goose Farm, therefore Wayne would be wise to have a minimum of wealth available for a judge to divide: would he like to pay for his solicitor's services in advance, approximately thirty thousand pounds? As for Diane, Wayne could not look after her, he was not qualified, so she must be taken into care – he, Morgan Chimbley, would arrange for the collection after a doctor had taken a drop of her blood.

Wayne said: 'Hold hard, Mr C – you people are meant to go slow, aren't you? Give me a breather, I'll tell you what's what next week.'

He plodded back to Goose Farm. He was no longer cheery. He was in a 'can't do' mood. Perhaps he drew the line at everything that should be done, according to his solicitor; or was it the kind of apathy to which members of his family were prone? He looked after Diane, she was not much trouble, which suited him.

But Diane seemed to take a hint. She suffered a 'cot death' in spite of Wayne's efforts to compensate for possibly being her father. She simplified his situation.

He booked a seat in Economy on a Magic Carpet flight to Australia – no Mile High fun and games, but dirt cheap.

48

On the day of departure he invested in the luxury of a taxi to Teasham, where he called at the bank and in a private room packed his rucksack with his fortune in packs of a thousand pounds, and on to Gatwick. The plane crashed over the Indian Ocean.

Mr Chimbley informed his wife, Heather. They were a busy couple, and only managed to talk privately at bedtime.

Heather was sorry to hear of the end of the Yockenthwaites.

'Poor little girl,' she remarked.

'Quite so – not his, I suspect – and not healthy – but a sad fate,' he agreed.

'What's happened to all that money?'

'Lost at sea.'

'What a waste!'

'Oh well – Wayne had the luck of the devil – inherited a fortune and died of a false economy – he booked seats on a cut-price airline – we'd better fly first class in future.'

'You're so funny, Morgan, you do make me laugh. Did you get properly paid for taking care of those millions?'

'Well, we had some good holidays, didn't we?'

'But they were business, weren't they?'

'Yes yes – my expenses were repaid.'

'Nothing more?'

'A little.'

'What's a little?'

'A quarter of a million.'

'Oh Morgan, what a clever hubby you are! I'm sorry all the same.'

'There may be more Yockenthwaite money in the offing. You don't have to worry too much about Wayne.'

'No, of course not. Would you like to celebrate, dear?'

Third Chapter of Nine

Time marched on, and the scene changed. Another farm in another county was inhabited by Yockenthwaites. There were six of them: old Wilfred and his wife Martha, their son Malcolm married to Catherina and their sons, John and Edmund. The home of these Yockenthwaites was in Norfolk, East Anglia, and the farm was called Windy Ridge.

It was as windy as its name, and often more so. Wind was normal, gales frequent, hurricanes occasional. The 'ridge' was rising ground on the edge of those erstwhile marshes now known as the Norfolk Broads. The farmhouse and farm buildings were seven miles from the North Sea, and there was nothing much between them and the Arctic Circle.

Trees had been planted in line for protection from the weather, evergreens, crab apples. They were meant to be hardy, but they were casualties, deformed by the pressure of zephyrs that were seldom gentle, poisoned by the salt in the air, partly leafless, often dead. Windy Ridge was lonely for obvious reasons, no one with any sense would build in its vicinity.

The stuff that had kept the farm standing on

its hillock for a good few centuries was flints, pebbles from the seashore that withstood rough treatment. All walls were made of unknapped flints, raw and rounded, set in thick mortar. In recent times roofs were made of corrugated iron bolted to joists and unable to fly away. The farmhouse tiles had been replaced by man or by God long ago, and the sheets of corrugated iron were rust-red and holed, but the Yockenthwaites did not object to a bucket or two in their attic.

The farm yielded a scanty living. These Yockenthwaites 'farmed' anything that would grow on their land, root vegetables mainly, and poultry in the sheds and barns. Their dependable crop was nettles and thistles. Their machinery sat about as if in retirement in the farmyard.

The head of the family, Wilfred, was an OAP – he had actually lived his three score years and ten. He had grizzled hair growing close to his scalp, a red face, a sharp nose, thin lips, whiskers because he shaved badly, hard blue eyes, and a stout and stolid physique. He looked agricultural in his boots, threadbare cords and jerseys, frayed shirts and greasy flat cap, but he had not done any agriculture – 'labouring' he called it – for many years; his work was 'mental'. He understood money, he made it, he could diddle with the best of them, he could pull a fast one and faster than most: those were his boasts. He bought and sold livestock and strips of land, rented out fields of his own, and tried to get Invalidity Benefit out of his doctor.

Malcolm, Wilfred's only child, now heading

for fifty years of age, was not shrewd like his father, he was dim verging on simple. He was not bad looking, but he had the rosy cheeks and unlined countenance of a person who does not think much. He was a 'labourer' and no mistake, he could dig a ditch and catch and kill a chicken, but he was defeated by the written word.

Malcolm's boys, Wilfred's grandsons, Eddy short for Edmund and Johnny long for John, were almost identical bumpkins and hayseeds. Eddy was a year older than Johnny. They were cleverer than their father, but were not adventurous, they tilled the land insofar as it was tillable and did not stray from Windy Ridge often. When they did, bicycling into Norwich or down to the beach, they stuck together and never got further than ogling the girls. They never had money to waste, they had only just enough to buy beer and cigarettes for themselves. Money for Malcolm was doled out by Wilfred, who kept a tight hold on the Yockenthwaite purse strings.

Wilfred's wife Martha was the archetypal countrywoman in old age. She was overweight, wore men's clothes more often than not, worked hard and long and stuck fast to a robotic schedule, slept eight hours every night, and cooked for the whole family as a rule.

Martha's daughter-in-law, Malcolm's wife Catherina, was the square peg, as her fancy name suggested. She was ugliness posing as beauty, and mutton dressed as lamb. She was big, tall, had dyed blonde hair hanging down her back, breasts that stuck out like blunt instruments, and a heavy undercarriage. She was chronically discontented. She scorned her husband publicly, she announced that he was impotent, she said she had never felt him making love to her. She mocked the Yockenthwaites behind their backs, and broadcast the fairy tale that she was going to spread her wings and fly to Paris. She and Malcolm occupied the cottage in close proximity to the pigstyes: she said it was like living in the toilet. She put up net curtains that resembled knickers, and called in workers at least to estimate for work on her cottage and perhaps to relieve her feelings. She had a spiteful tongue and scrapped with her in-laws at every opportunity. Her marriage must have been a bed of nails for Malcolm; luckily he did not know the meanings of the worst words she hurled at him.

Sundays differed from the Yockenthwaites' weekdays, although they were not churchgoing. They ate breakfast together at eight-thirty instead of six-thirty. They congregated ten minutes early so as not to spoil the food, and sat on hard chairs at the pine refectory table. Martha fried eggs from their fowls, salty bacon from their pigs, fried bread, fried potatoes, field mushrooms, and black pudding if the butcher had had any. Cereals were on offer, and coffee and hot milk. Relays of toast were served, and pots of marmalade and strawberry jam, and half-pound slabs of butter.

On a particular Sunday Martha kept on frying, the men attacked their victuals like wolves, and

Catherina held forth on the side-effects of stuffing oneself with food.

When they had done eating, Eddy half-rose from his chair, reached under himself, withdrew a tattered newspaper, and said: 'Grandad, got your glasses? Read what's written here. I've ringed it with black.'

Wilfred told his grandson to do the reading.

'Listen, then,' Eddy began; '"Yockenthwaite, Any blood relation of Shadrach or Wayne Yockenthwaite should contact Chimbley Chimbley and Davis, full address below, and will hear something to his or her advantage."'

Suitable exclamations followed.

Wilfred asked: 'Where you get the paper?'

Eddy and Johnny exchanged glances and laughed.

Eddy explained sheepishly: 'My ma, she wants us to go in the garden. We don't mind, though it can be draughty. Anyhow, I was tearing up paper to hang on the nail in the privy. I was sitting and looking at a bit of paper and read the name. It was yesterday. What do you think, Grandad?'

There was some laughter. Johnny said, 'Lucky it wasn't used', and Martha, 'More breakfast, anyone?'

Wilfred spoke.

'Could be money there.'

Malcolm asked: 'How's that, Dad?' – and was ignored.

Catherina's question was more to the point.

'Are you related to those Yockenthwaites?'

Wilfred replied: 'Could be. I heard tell of that

name when I was a boy. I'd claim to be related to King Kong for ready money. No, no,' he corrected himself, 'this is business, no joke. My pa talked of Shadback. Well spotted, Eddy!'

'Shadrach,' Catherina edged in like a schoolmistress.

Martha said: 'What a funny thing!'

Johnny said: 'What's to be done?'

Eddy said: 'Yes, Grandad, what are you going to do?'

'Oh I'll follow it up, no doubt about that, tomorrow morning, Monday, or soon enough. I'll do as I've told you to do – never pass a penny on the pavement.'

Catherina was heard to say to her Malcolm as the breakfast party split up: 'You keep the old fool up to it – don't let him forget – and don't you forget either!'

Forty-eight hours later Wilfred rang Chimbley Chimbley and Davis and was put through to Mr Morgan Chimbley.

'You have the right name, sir,' Mr Chimbley told him, 'but you would have to undergo a DNA test before I could speak of the advantage mentioned in my advertisement. Do you know what a DNA test is?'

'That I do – have to be sure bulls are the right ones before you let them loose.'

'Quite so. You'd have to give your drop of blood on one day, and I could tell you the result on the day following. Which Yockenthwaite do you think you're connected with?'

'Shadback.'

'Yes – Shadrach – like the man in the Bible – but he was not so lucky as his namesake – he perished in a fire.'

'Perished, did he?'

'The cause of death was a heart attack.'

'Who burnt him?'

'He must have started the fire himself.'

'What he do that for?'

'I don't know, Mr Yockenthwaite. But we're straying from the point. I imagine you'll be coming down to Teasham and staying the night while the DNA test is done. I can recommend our local hotel, the Drum and Monkey.'

'No hotel – we'll do as we please, if you don't mind. You give us a date!'

The date was fixed, and Wilfred informed his wife in front of his family.

He said to Martha: 'I'll be driving down to Gloucestershire. Johnny can drive me. Maybe I'll win the money to pay for the petrol. We'll have to stay the night. When did I last do that, Mother?'

Martha replied: 'Can't remember you ever did. You've kept me awake with your snoring ever since we shared a bed.'

They departed in the old Volvo. Johnny was at the wheel, Wilfred beside him with a basketful of food. The Volvo was the family car, still in working order but no longer luxurious inside – it had carried pigs to market. It took them most of a day to reach Teasham and find the surgery of the doctor engaged by Mr Chimbley to do the blood job. Wilfred and Johnny then looked round for a B&B. They discovered a couple, but Wilfred said they were too pricey, and he and his grandson ended up by eating the remainder of their rations and sleeping in the car.

In the morning Wilfred said he was sick of all the palaver and would have liked to go home, but Johnny urged him to see things through. They reported to the offices of Chimbley Chimbley and Davis at ten o'clock.

Mr Morgan Chimbley greeted them promptly, ushered them into his office and, when they were seated, said: 'Mr Yockenthwaite, you are a true Yockenthwaite, and you have inherited seven and a half million pounds.'

Wilfred passed out.

They feared he had passed over, but Mr Chimbley took the liberty of slapping his cheeks, Johnny yanked him back on to his chair, an employee of the solicitors forced water between his blue lips, and he came to. It was brief, his first recovery of consciousness: Johnny shouted into his ear, 'You're near eight million richer,' and his eyes turned up and he was out for another five minutes. But then he seemed to be himself, he spoke no worse than usual, and reacted more or less typically to his change of fortune.

'Seven million,' he repeated in a marvelling tone of voice, then asked with a crafty wink: 'Where's the money coming from and what's the catch?'

Mr Chimbley replied: 'You are the heir of

your relative, Shadrach Yockenthwaite. He won a large sum of money in a lottery, invested it in dated deposit accounts worldwide, one of which has matured and is paying out seven-plus million pounds. The bank that has dealt with this portion of your inheritance is in Azerbaijan, and there is no catch. You inherit not only money, also a place called Goose Farm down here in Gloucestershire, a house with a smallholding of somewhat unrewarding land. Your money is at present in the safe keeping of the NatWest Bank across the street, where the manager, Mr Burns, is waiting to make your acquaintance.'

'Well I never!'

'Good news, Grandad,' Johnny exclaimed.

'Don't you count your chickens,' Wilfred warned.

Mr Chimbley spoke: 'There is a bill for tax.'

'I do not like that word, Mr Chimney, I hate it.'

'Chimbley, if you please, sir.'

'Oh, beg pardon. What's the damage?'

'Your relation's winnings were not taxed, but the Inland Revenue has ruled that his bequests are to be liable for death duty at the current rate.'

'How much?'

'Forty per cent.'

'In money?'

'Three million – three and a quarter million, all told.'

'Hear that, Johnny? What did I say?'

'I'm sorry, Mr Yockenthwaite...'

'Oh I won't pay.'

'It's the law.'

'Not my law – I don't hold with your laws – I don't believe in taxes – I never paid tax.'

'Mr Yockenthwaite, your money is in my name at this moment. I cannot release to you the money you owe me, for example.'

'What are you charging me for?'

'Shadrach's primary heir was his grandson, Wayne by name, actually an Australian. He met with an unfortunate accident, I regret to say, he was one of the fatalities of a plane crash over the Indian Ocean. I therefore had to register his death in both England and with the Australian authorities. Furthermore, I have maintained the fabric of Goose Farm, paid builders and agricultural specialists for running repairs and upkeep of land and fences, and ordered two valuations of the property. And I have travelled to Switzerland to try once more to obtain information from the Maria Theresa Bank, which seems to be involved in the distribution of the total wealth of your relative.'

Wilfred responded to this speech by means of an odd gurgling noise. Johnny patted him on the back with considerable force, and he shook his head, said to his grandson, 'Hold off, boy!' and then addressed Mr Chimbley.

'What was that, sir? What did you say?'

'I expect you mean the total wealth?'

'I did, I do – that could be a good bit more than seven?'

'It could, Mr Yockenthwaite, I agree.'

'So where is it?'

'I don't know. Nobody knows to the best of our knowledge.'

'You're not sitting on it, like?'

'I am not. All I can tell you is that you have a chance of inheriting more than the money waiting for you in the bank.'

'By golly! Damn and blast! What about your luck, Johnny, being my son? But that's future, Mr Chimbley, ain't it? That's maybe! I'm methodical, see, and put first things first. You want to get your hand in the bran-tub. How much your charges add up to?'

'Including a fortnight in Switzerland, and another investigative journey to the Cayman Islands, where Wayne's money came from, some two hundred and fifty thousand pounds.'

'A quarter of a million?'

'Approximately.'

'See that, Johnny? Better money than farming. You be a solicitor, and you'll keep us all in our old age. How come, Mr Chimbley?'

'I can give you my itemised account.'

'Are you a married man?'

'Yes. Why?'

'Take your wife with you to foreign parts?'

'Mr Yockenthwaite, if you wish to lodge a complaint against my firm, I can give you a form to fill in, it will have to be sent to our governing organisation in London, it will take time to be processed, and I could not hand over your money until the matter was settled.'

'That's how the land lies, does it?' Well, you

tell me this, how much an hour, Mr Chimbley? Throw me a bone to get my teeth into.'

'Three hundred and fifty pounds.'

'For one hour?'

'Precisely.'

'Good for you, Mr Chimbley! I never did, I never heard the like! In daylight, too! Mr Chimbley, I'll be saying goodbye. I don't want no more talk with you at a tenner a word.'

'Please sit down, Mr Yockenthwaite. We have other business to transact. In view of your attitude to my remuneration, I shall stop the clock now and continue to offer my advice scot-free.'

'What other business?'

'Goose Farm, I have the keys of Goose Farm here in my desk. What shall I do with them?'

'They're mine, aren't they?'

'They are.'

'Thank you then.'

A horny hand reached out and the keys were dropped into it.

'Mr Yockenthwhaite, your family – could you tell me how many dependents you have?'

'Family, is it?'

'Yes, please.'

'Wife Martha, and son Malcolm and his wife, Catherina, and their two sons, this one, Johnny, and his brother, Eddy.'

'Let me see, they would be five in number, and they are now your heirs presumptive, each could inherit from you in certain sad circumstances. I take it you have not yet made a will?'

'That's paperwork – I steer clear of paperwork.'

'In the event of your death, as things stand, your wife would inherit your money, Goose Farm and Windy Ridge, your land, livestock, and so on.'

'My Martha wouldn't want it, she doesn't know nothing, she'd let it go to Malcolm.'

'In that case gift tax would be levied.'

'Don't talk tax to me, Mr Chimney.'

'Very well. But I insist on telling you that you should make a will without delay, and indicate how your property should be divided and which member of your family should inherit what.'

'You can save your breath. I've dealt with money all my life, I don't need advice. I'll just collect the banknotes now, and be getting off home.'

'Mr Yockenthwaite, your money isn't in banknotes, millionaires don't carry their money in banknotes. You'll have to make arrangements with Mr Burns to transfer your money to your local branch of the NatWest, and order cheque books. I would add before we go across to the bank that I would be most willing to draft a will for you and send it to you in Norfolk. I could do that as soon as you inform me of your wishes.'

'I heard you.'

'Finally, Mr Yockenthwaite, the tax outstanding – may I deduct it from the seven and a half million pounds?'

'You may not.'

'Excuse me?'

'I do not excuse you. I'm not having any deductions. You can send me your bill, and wait till I pay it. The taxman gets the big O. You excuse me, Mr Chimbley, for blurting out you've still to learn I mean what I say.'

They went to the bank, the solicitor and the two Yockenthwaites. Mr Burns tried to express his fondness for Shadrach and Wayne, but Wilfred cut him short. Wilfred had suffered more jawjaw than he could bear: he was never a good listener, he detested people who knew more than he did, he was now in a position to shut traps, he had a lot of thinking to do and he wanted to do it at home. He accepted a statement of his account, an offer to transfer money over to Norfolk, a debit card, cheque books, half a dozen leaflets, and withdrew a hundred pounds and said ta and then ta-ta.

He and Johnny headed for the car park. Johnny mentioned a meal, he implied that they could afford one, but his grandad opted for two sandwiches and a couple of cans of Coke from a kiosk, and they climbed into the Volvo and thundered eastward.

Wilfred did not eat all his sandwich. He gave half of it to Johnny, and fell asleep. He was not himself. Of course he was not, he was millions of pounds richer, he was no longer a poor old money-grubber, he was rich – all the same, Johnny wondered if he had gone peculiar after passing out like that.

Johnny drove and Wilfred snored for several hours. When the soft western air changed into

64

inland polluted and then into bracing ozone, and the skies grew bigger – in other words they were back in Norfolk – Wilfred roused himself and Johnny asked a question.

'Grandad, if you won't pay tax, how you going to keep in the clear?'

'I'll let sleeping dogs lie.'

A family pow-wow ensued. The news that they were millionaires was broken. They had to have teas and coffees to help them to take it in. There was also back-slapping. Catherina ran true to form. She asked if her father-in-law would share the money out.

'I'm not telling no one nothing, not yet,' Wilfred replied.

Eddy said: 'There are four of us, that's two million each if you divide by four.'

Catherina was not wearing it.

'Thank you, Eddy, for forgetting your mother. I know women are less than flies in the Yockenthwaite family, but I have rights and I know them, and I will not be ruled out of getting a single penny of these undeserved riches.'

Eddy accepted the challenge.

'Oh Mother, I'll see you get your penny, don't fret, you'll be able to go in the public toilet.'

Johnny teased his mother by saying: 'Are you wanting Gran to have an equal share, along with you and us four men?'

There was laughter at Martha's expense.

Luckily she missed the point.

She said: 'I don't know what you're all talking about. If Grandad's got money, it's his, isn't it? I've never got money out of him, and I can't see why anybody else should – until he dies, that's to say.'

More laughter.

'I'm not dead,' Wilfred growled.

Catherina crossed another dividing line between good and bad taste.

She said: 'Well, Father-in-law, you mustn't forget you had a turn in Gloucestershire – you fainted in the solicitor's office – and that's an omen – I just hope you've made your will and remembered that my Malcolm is your rightful heir. If you won't share while you're alive, I hope you'll do the right thing afterwards.'

Malcolm told his wife to 'shut it'. He said it in a way that would provoke her. He said: 'Shut your big mouth, Catherine, can't you?' She hated to be called by the name she was christened with – and she rounded on her husband.

'Why were you sitting on your hands when we were told about the money? You should have been staking your claim. You're so feeble, Malcolm, you're a flop.'

At this point both her sons, Eddy and Johnny, rose in defence of their father.

'Don't be rude, Mother ... Get a hold of your tongue, Ma, or I will!'

Wilfred called for order, silence, and stopping all the nonsense, and temporarily he was successful.

But at the next meeting the subject of Goose Farm popped up for discussion. The boys, Eddy and Johnny, said it could not be left to rot, a house with land was worth more than peanuts, and could one of them have it?

'If I did that,' Wilfred countered, 'who'd do the work round here?'

Malcolm offered to do the work of two.

Wilfred hurt his feelings by saying: 'Your work don't count.'

And then they were off again, Catherina standing up for the husband she herself continually laid low, both boys threatening to go and live in Goose Farm, and Martha chipping in with the remark that Goose Farm was for geese, not Yockenthwaites.

Another armistice broke out. Wilfred did some thinking, and proved it by talking to himself more than usual, muttering and shaking his head. He coped irritably with actions that could be compared with guerrilla warfare: lists of needs being pressed into his hands or left on his place at the table in the kitchen. Martha listed new cooking pots; Catherina was after new windows and a new set of net curtains – the ones that looked like her knickers had holes in the wrong places; and Eddy wished for better gates for the farmland, and Johnny for a replacement of the Volvo.

Wilfred ignored everything. He sat out of doors, pondering, and indoors, during meals, he would raise his hands negatively or cover his ears. But he had to receive letters, important ones, it seemed, in brown envelopes or even registered. They were cursed and soon torn up, some without being opened. He was watched by the members of his family, who were concerned for his health, concerned for his money, and especially in case he was going crackers.

Financially, life went on as before at Windy Ridge. Money was as tight as ever, while the millions mouldered in one branch or another of the NatWest. Nobody had the nerve to challenge the authority of Wilfred, or make sense of the situation. The idea that he might be certifiable was reinforced when telephone calls, two or three, noteworthy happenings at the home of the Yockenthwaites, followed the letters, and an outdoor telephone wire was found to be cut.

A visitor was a still rarer occurrence. A middle-aged man in a pinstripe suit arrived by taxi at Windy Ridge, spent a quarter of an hour with Wilfred, and departed in the same taxi.

Johnny recognised him. Johnny spilt the beans. At supper he requested information.

'What was Mr Chimbley doing here, Grandad?'

'You mind your business,' Wilfred grunted.

But Martha, Malcolm and Catherina, and Eddy were also present, and they swooped on the exchange like vultures.

'The solicitor ... All the way from Teasham ... Is he the person who's been writing letters ... Was he at the other end of the telephone calls ... It must be serious ... We have a right to know ... Why all the mystery ... And where's the money ... Why are you hiding it... Have you spent it ... What's going on?'

'Money's safe as it ever was,' Wilfred announced.

The vultures were far from satisfied.

'Where's it gone ... Are we ruined?'

'The taxman's fined us. Taxman wants nearly half of what we've got. Now he's taken more, because I wouldn't pay.'

'How much ... What's the damage ... What are the figures?'

Johnny had his say.

'I know Inland Revenue wanted three million, I heard it talked about.'

The others were aghast. They reacted as Wilfred had to the proposition that a bureaucrat in London could snaffle three whole million pounds from anyone legally. There were panicky murmurs: '... They can't ... Don't pay ... It's thieving.'

But Wilfred shouted down the babble.

'Listen! I wasn't paying no death duty. I wouldn't go back on my word. So taxman's piled another two hundred thousand on my bill. It's gone up from three million to three million seven hundred thousand. That's the sober truth. And next time, if I didn't pay, solicitor says it'd be over four mill.'

A short silence fell.

Malcolm asked with his customary smile: 'That's done it, Pa.'

'You're not far wrong for a change.' Wilfred snapped at him. 'I've done it. I've wrote the cheque.'

Eddy commented: 'Had to be, Grandad.'

Catherina moved the conversation forward.

'Does this mean you can distribute the millions that are left?'

Wilfred answered: 'It does not. You're too impatient, you are. You stop the clock by hanging out that tongue of yours, Catherina.'

Martha said: 'I'll fetch in the pudding.'

It was judged to be humorous. The two boys laughed at their Gran, and Malcolm had a snigger. Even Wilfred had to smile.

'You do that, Mother. I could fancy a bit of sweet,' he said.

The problems in the plural of Windy Ridge were not solved.

The Yockenthwaites were not in debt, but they were in a mess. Obviously, Wilfred could not reach a decision in respect of the future of his four millions, and might never be fit to do so. The potential heirs grew more resentful of skimping and penny-pinching – no longer an example of the injustice of fate but a whim of Wilfred Yockenthwaite; and avarice led to outbursts of ill humour, violent language and tantrums.

Catherina dared to call her father-in-law a selfish old billy goat, if only in an undertone. Eddy demanded to know: 'Done your will yet?' Johnny had words with his grandad over harvesting the kale: 'Can't manage without more help.'

Wilfred's reaction was so stupid as to add to the suspicions that he was not all there. He went back to labouring. He was out in the fields in the bad weather, not making money, not counting his money, not sharing it out. One day he and Malcolm and the two boys were cutting the kale. Wilfred had joined in, although it was rough work and dirty – the kale stood tall and the big leaves caught the rainwater. Wilfred had been bending down to cut the stalks in one line, and he did not stand up. Malcolm called his name – no answer. Eddy walked over and found his grandad on the ground, warm but dead, no mistaking it.

They carried him into the house. Martha was bemused by the sight of her moribund spouse. She could only say: 'He ate a good breakfast, too.' Catherina was summoned and rang for a doctor. She then said they had to notify Chimbley Chimbley and Davis, and persuaded Johnny to run her down to the village where she could use the public telephone. Doctor Haycroft arrived at Windy Ridge – he had been there before, called out by Catherina to heal the wounds to her nervous system; and the white van of the undertakers came and went.

Catherina returned. She explained that she had also spoken to Mr James, a manager at the Norwich branch of the NatWest. She was agitated, much more so than she had been by Wilfred's death. She told Malcolm and their sons, Eddy and Johnny, the reason why.

Definitely no will – Wilfred intestate – the money belonged to Martha – and the millions were now untouchable, out of reach, until all the legal requirements were over and done with – family would have to live on a line of credit she had obtained from the bank.

She did have an answer to the next question. If a second death tax was to be avoided, possibly

71

avoided, Martha would have to refuse to accept her inheritance. It was a faint hope. Malcolm was now the heir presumptive, and he – the husband of Catherina – must not be shy of telling his mother that he, not she, should have all the money, that it was her duty to save millions of pounds from the clutches of a greedy government and, instead, place them where they belonged, in the hands of her son and grandchildren. Catherina wasted no time in conveying this message, and half-convincing Malcolm and the boys that they would be right to get round the wrong of a tax on innocence. She insisted, she nagged night and day until the funeral and for a week or two afterwards.

At last Malcolm agreed to have a shot at it. But to suggest that he drew a blank would be an understatement. His mother understood nothing, except that she would never ever go against Wilfred or his works. She would not sign her name on any piece of paper. She would not listen to naughty arguments. She was never one for money, she said, as everybody should be, not grabby, like Catherina in particular. Malcolm was not worth listening to, and he was to leave her in peace.

Eddy had a go, Johnny followed. Gran would not budge. Mr Chimbley was asked to come to the rescue, expense notwithstanding. He failed. Catherina, metaphorically, attacked her mother-in-law with bare knuckles. The consequences were not quite intended, and negative in every sense. Martha suffered a seizure after Catherina had finished with her, and lost the power of speech and the use of her right hand.

They tried to keep her alive. They nursed her for all they were worth, or, rather, she was. But she expired, and cost her heir a full two mill, including the solicitor's expenses.

Malcolm was not too badly off. He was a millionaire, and the owner of Windy Ridge and Goose Farm. But coming into money had a worrying effect on him and his attitude. He had been downtrodden by his father and his wife, at school, at work, and even by his sons. He was a fool, and had been called one so often that he ceased to disagree with the description. But remarkably, almost overnight, he underwent a transformation, his fairy godmother waved her wand, and he realised he had become a somebody. He did not have so much money as his father, but it was enough, more than he would have dreamed of if he had ever had a dream. And he was not the worried one, he was less worried than ever before. The worriers were Catherina and Eddy and Johnny. They could not get hold of Malcolm's money. They could not beg or borrow the housekeeping money without a row. Their worst worry was that he would squander it in one weird way or another, and there would be none for any of those who deserved it.

Self-interest complicated the story. At first Catherina and her sons presented a united front to Malcolm. Their cry was that he had to share and share alike – it was the right, proper, good and nice thing for him to do. Malcolm was unmoved. Then Catherina reverted to browbeating her husband according to custom, and threatened to cut his throat if he should give money to the boys. The boys grasped the precariousness of their footholds on the golden rock-face. They made common cause against their mother, entreating their father to hand over at least presents, at most a percentage, before a greedy person got the lot. But Eddy went behind Johnny's back to remind Malcolm that he was the first-born and should have more than his brother. Johnny, discovering treachery, told his father that Eddy was dishonest and money-mad, while he on the other hand was straight and would look after Malcolm in his old age.

The atmosphere at Windy Ridge, in the farmhouse Malcolm and Catherina had moved into, where Eddy and Johnny spent more time than usual, watching TV as well as eating there, watching their father and not going upstairs to bed until he did, the very air in the old house turned nasty. Malcolm slowly came round to understanding that he was not popular. He deduced that he was doing wrong, whatever wrong was. He missed meals in order not to be stared at with hostility. No one was kind to him any more. He worked harder to try to please, more than antisocial hours, an escapist schedule. Before too long he died of it. Money had not saved him from a cold that mutated into flu, pleurisy, pneumonia, high fever and a lethal cardiac infarction, otherwise known as a heart attack.

No will, of course. His next of kin was his wife. Catherina had been well aware of her prospects, and had not made a fuss about his intestacy: she bullied him about everything else, but was afraid that in a will he would make a mess of his money and divide it. She took what she got, not with a good grace, she blamed Malcolm for having proved to be a miser when he was rich, and an idiot before that, but she could not complain of having a million in her large red hands. She told her sons in no uncertain terms that she was not giving any of it away and was also hanging on to the two properties, Norfolk and Gloucestershire, as she called them pretentiously.

The quarrels with her sons drove her abroad. She played the injured mother just as she had played the injured wife. And she played other games in Las Vegas and Monaco. Eddy and Johnny tilled the barren soil of Windy Ridge. They were hard up, hard done by, bitter, angry, and without expectations. They did not bother to complain to Mr Chimbley – he knew no more than they did, so he said. Their mother was incommunicado, she had vanished and forgotten them. They could see no trace of a blue sky, and time dragged from one year to the next.

The news of their mother's demise was a happy release neither for herself, she was only in her late fifties, nor for her sons, who were informed that she had been nearly broke. They rejected Mr Chimbley's offer to come to Norfolk to tie up loose ends, they could not afford his kindness. And no, their mother was not to be brought home, she could be buried as cheaply as possible in Nevada, and they would not be attending the funeral.

Mr Chimbley wrote a letter nonetheless. It ran: 'Dear Edmund and John, May I offer condolences for the death of your mother, Catherina Yockenthwaite? The losses of mother, father and grandparents in a relatively short space of time must leave you heavy-hearted. With regret, I can shed light on the financial picture. The Inland Revenue claimed forty per cent of three fortunes, thus seven and a half million pounds was reduced to the million that your mother inherited from your father. She spent that inheritance in America, then raised money by mortgaging Windy Ridge, which probably now belongs to the company she dealt with. She was actually trying to borrow against the value of Goose Farm in her last days; but she did not succeed partly because of her timing, partly because Goose Farm is so dilapidated as to be almost valueless. As you will see from the above, you two brothers inherit what will be virtually nil after the deducation of my firm's fees. You are, however, heirs presumptive of Shadrach Yockenthwaite, you are in line to gain from his estate. In my considered opinion, you might have to wait years to receive such money, and you could never receive it. Shadrach was an unpredictable man, and could have played all sorts of tricks with his wealth, leaving it to strangers, for instance. I therefore have a proposal to lay before you. I would be prepared to pay each of you a modest sum if you would sign a waiver of your future rights to the Yockenthwaite estate. I spoke of such a waiver before – to your mother, I think it was, and with reference to your grandmother. In your own case, I would urge your acceptance of five hundred pounds apiece without delay rather than nothing now and conceivably more on one of those elusive fine days. Sincerely yours, Morgan Chimbley.'

The brothers took the money and signed on for work on a merchant ship berthed at Tilbury and sailing to the Far East.

Morgan Chimbley reported this satisfactory outcome to his wife, Heather.

'I pity the family,' she said. 'How dare the government tax people twice over, once when they're alive and again when they die?'

'Very true, dear,' he said.

'How generous of you to give your earnings to the two young men. What a husband I have! You didn't give away all the money you earned, Morgan?'

'Not quite, dear.'

'I'm glad. How much did you give them? I wouldn't like to think you were out of pocket.'

'A tidy sum, shall we say.'

'I hope they were grateful.'

'The arrangement is mutually beneficial. The boys have a chance to earn real money and I shall be well paid when Shadrach's next consignment of gold arrives. Yockenthwaites are not to be trusted with money, they seem to have no financial sense.'

'I think it's much safer in your hands, Morgan.'

'Well, yes, I would have to agree with you.'

Fourth Chapter of Nine

Mr Chimbley sat behind the desk in his office with its black tin boxes piled high, and a man in late middle age, bespectacled, bald, thin and shabbily dressed, sat on the edge of a chair on the other side of the desk.

The latter, Alfred Collins, who claimed to be a Yockenthwaite in all but name, had flown to England from South Africa, submitted to a DNA test, and was now waiting to hear the news 'considerably to his advantage' that he had read about in a newspaper.

Mr Chimbley spoke.

'I'm pleased to be able to tell you that the test has proved you are who you have said you are. You are a Yockenthwaite, Mr Collins. Your relationship with Shadrach of Goose Farm entitles you to inherit a large estate. The bricks and mortar and the land consist of the aforesaid Goose Farm and the money is in excess of twenty million pounds.'

Mr Collins sat back on his chair, he crumpled backwards, raised a hand to cover his eyes and, as if to ward off a blow, groaned twice, 'Oh no, oh no!'

'My apologies for having kept you on

tenterhooks, sir,' Mr Chimbley said; 'but I'm sure you realise I have had to be wary of imposters. I understand that your relationship with Shadrach is through a grandparent, and that you never met him, your benefactor. I have been told he was a solitary individual, almost a hermit in his old age, and not flush with money when he won a monetary prize in a sweepstake of sorts. He then deposited his money in tax havens all round the world, in accounts that were dated to mature in a succession of years – that is, to pay over the capital. Two large sums have already reached me and been passed on to Yockenthwaites who would be your cousins, a Wayne from Australia and a Wilfred from East Anglia.'

'Were they entitled?' Mr Collins asked in a faint voice.

'They were, they were genuine Yockenthwaites.'

'If so, why aren't they getting the money you say I'm getting?'

Mr Chimbley cleared his throat.

'Mr Wayne had an unfortunate accident.'

'How unfortunate?'

'He lost his life flying back to Australia.'

'What was the name of the other heir?'

'Wilfred.'

'That's it.'

'He is no longer with us, and the same applies to his wife, son and daughter-in-law. The two grandsons are also not with us in a financial sense.'

'Excuse me?'

'Three of Wilfred's heirs died in quick succession. The death duties payable on three demises,

Wilfred's and two others, were tragic inasmuch as the grandsons inherited almost negative bequests. They decided to emigrate to the Far East and to search for better luck out there. They both signed documents indicating that they were waiving all their rights to any more of Shadrach's money that might emerge. The documents were witnessed and have been proved legally. I am therefore at liberty to pass Shadrach's latest consignment of treasure to yourself.'

'Is this consignment the last?'

'I don't know, sir. Shadrach's intention must have been to conceal his money from prying eyes. The first two consignments came from the Cayman Islands and Azerbaijan respectively and yours from Dubai.'

'What complications! Were they worthwhile?'

'That's debatable. I have to inform you that death duty will be levied on your inheritance.'

'What's that?'

'Forty per cent, eight million pounds in your case.'

'My head's spinning, Mr Chimbley. I entered this room of yours a poor man, and now you're telling me I have to surrender eight millions of my money to the government. I don't believe in wasting money, I don't!'

'You betray a characteristic of the Yockenthwaite family by what you say, sir. Shadrach was the opposite of a wastrel.'

'But I'm to be a multimillionaire even after losing eight million?'

'Do you regret it, Mr Collins?'

'How can I say so? How could I be so un-grateful?'

'Forgive me, sir. I know next to nothing of your circumstances. You have been domiciled at Peak Holding, near Durban, South Africa. Is that a country property?'

'It's a smallholding. We emigrated to South Africa because life was cheaper there, and we hoped to earn money. But we hoped in vain.'

'You are a married man, Mr Collins?'

'My wife Hermione has put up with a lot.'

'Was there issue?'

'Beg pardon?'

'Do you have children?'

Mr Collins seemed to jump uneasily.

'Two boys,' he said.

'What age are they?'

'George is twenty-one, Davey's eighteen.'

'Where are they?'

'At home, at Peak Holding with my wife.'

'Do they work on your land?'

'George does – there's not much land – Davey doesn't.'

'Will your family move into Goose Farm, do you think?'

'Oh yes – bound to – nothing worth waiting for in South Africa.'

'They know you're here, and why you are?'

'I should say so!'

'How will they respond to your good fortune?'

Mr Collins produced a tissue and began to mop his brow. He was speechless and bent forwards with his head down.

'Are you in trouble?' Mr Chimbley asked.

'I'll be all right.'

'Can I help?'

'A glass of water, please.'

Mr Chimbley walked over to the door, ordered the water, and brought it to Mr Collins, who had regained his composure.

'Are you able to continue our conversation?'

'Oh yes.'

'I hope I said nothing to upset you.'

'You have upset me – not your fault.'

'I'm sorry, sir. I was asking you about your family response to your good news.'

'Yes.'

'I'm sure they'll be overjoyed.'

'My wife ... My sons are ... My sons are not compatible. I have concerns in that area.'

'How would you wish to proceed, Mr Collins?'

'What do you mean?'

'Money sets you free in one way and in another is a ball and chain. Your money is in an account in our local NatWest bank, and the manager, Mr Burns, will be pleased to assist you with banking decisions at your earliest convenience. You should also, if I may suggest it, make a will, unless you wish your entire fortune to pass to Mrs Collins. Perhaps you would like to rest and accustom yourself to your changed situation. Where are you staying at present? Would you like to go straight out to Goose Farm – I could accompany you with the keys? Alternatively, you might like to move into an hotel.'

'Oh dear!'

'Don't let me rush you, sir. Solicitors are taught to take their time.'

'I'm not a well man.'

'Did you say you're not well, sir?'

'I'm not up to being so rich.'

'Come come, Mr Collins! You can now afford to pay the very best doctors.'

'Too late for that.'

'I'm sorry.'

'So am I.'

'Your decisions, sir?'

'I'm not sure I've been lucky.'

'Pardon?'

'Is there a curse on this money?'

'No, sir, no – money isn't a curse, it's a blessing.'

'The blessing's killed my relations.'

'They died, sir, they weren't killed.'

'Was that the verdict? I must study the evidence – not a lot of difference often – I'm thinking of the members of my own immediate family.'

'Indeed?'

'Take no notice, I was talking to myself.'

'Well, I'm sure you and Mrs Collins and your sons will have long lives in which to enjoy great wealth.'

'Anyway, they won't have to kill me.'

'Mr Collins! Dear me! I admit the Yockenthwaite blood is not so pure as driven snow, but to my knowledge it has never strayed in the direction of homicide.'

'The wealth is mine, no strings attached?'

'It is, sir.'

'No chance of an argument over who it belongs to?'

'None.'

'And my will, no one would discover its contents until I am in another world?'

'The only copy, if you would prefer not to have it photocopied, will be kept in our strongroom until that unhappy occasion.'

'Could be a happy one.'

Mr Chimbley coughed.

'Would you be ready to instruct me here and now?'

'Why not?'

'I have my pen and paper at the ready, sir.'

'Will you confirm that I will inherit twelve million?'

'I confirm that you have inherited twelve million pounds approximately and before deductions.'

'My money is to be divided between three heirs.'

'Your wife, and your sons George and Davey – naturally. Is Davey a pet name or a Christian name?'

'The latter, oddly enough.'

'I shall write it as Davey. Will the division be into three equal parts?'

'No, decidedly not! The bulk is to go to George.'

'What is the bulk?'

'Ten million pounds.'

Mr Chimbley cleared his throat.

'A very large percentage,' he remarked.

'George deserves it.'

'Your wife, sir?'

'One million.'

'And Davey?'

'One million.'

'Are you sure of these figures, Mr Collins?'

'Yes.'

'Are they fair, sir?'

'Yes.'

'They could lead to litigation.'

'So what?'

'A legal challenge and claim by your wife and your younger son could be extremely unpleasant.'

'Oh, they'll challenge all right, but George will have the wherewithal to keep their lawyers at bay, if he has the stomach for a fight. Can you render my will as resistant to challenges as possible?'

'I can.'

'And I can trust you, Mr Chimbley?'

'Absolutely, sir.'

'How long will it take you to draw up the document? I would like to sign it today.'

'Two hours, sir.'

'Very well. I'd like to go to the bank.'

'I will introduce you to Mr Burns.'

'Thank you. Tell me about Goose Farm. Is it habitable?'

'Yes – damp but with the services connected – you will find electric fires and an electric cooker, and water available. I have maintained it personally while it's been empty.'

'Mr Chimbley, I have some shopping to do.

After meeting Mr Burns, I need to see a doctor. And I suppose I need to buy a little food, and must pay my bill where I stayed last night. I'll then return for the signing and witnessing of my will. Lastly, may I accept your offer to drive me out to Goose Farm?'

'You will be alone there, sir. Are you against going to an hotel?'

'I like to be alone for a change, and I may not be for long.'

'Of course, your family will be joining you.'

'Yes, though not exactly what I meant.'

The funeral of Mr Alfred Collins-Yockenthwaite occurred at Lilacvale Crematorium in Teasham. He had survived until his family joined him at Goose Farm, he actually died in the night of the day of their arrival. Two non-family mourners were in the chapel with the coffin, which was in line with the red velvet curtain across the hatch to nether regions. Mr Chimbley and Mr Burns sat together at the back. A priest in a white surplice sat on a chair at the front, waiting to start the service. Melancholy musak played.

Raised voices heralded the entry of a dumpy woman in a hat, hair red and dry-looking, face much made up, followed by a tall youth with a benevolent expression on his regular facial features, and a small individual with shoulder-length hair and eyebrows that met over his reddish nose. They were the widow, the elder son and the younger son of the deceased, Hermione, George and Davey. They had been arguing outside the chapel – Hermione had been clearly heard to say, 'Please! Please!' – as if asking for respect.

George carried a bunch of flowers and laid them on the coffin. The professional men exchanged a critical glance. The flowers were mostly wild ones, weeds really, and not what could have been expected from a family worth twenty million gross.

The service began. Davey was restless and seemed to be impatient. He looked over his shoulder twice to smile at the solicitor and banker. A hymn was sung mainly by the priest, a few prayers were spoken, the coffin slid through the velvet curtain, and the family turned to leave with no outward signs of grief. The time was four-thirty, tea time. Mrs Collins-Yockenthwaite, on the way out, invited Mr Chimbley and Mr Burns to a cup of tea at Goose Farm.

Her invitation was crude: 'One of you has the will, and the other's got the money – right, isn't it? – you'll both be welcome at the hovel we live in – we can offer you English tea or a drop of hooch if that's your fancy.'

Mr Chimbley drove out alone, Mr Burns had thought it would not be discreet for him to be in on the terms of the will. He drove slowly to give the family a chance to prepare the so-called wake, and avoided with difficulty several new potholes in the Goose Farm drive.

The atmosphere in the house was hostile and tense. The interested parties sat round the fireplace in the sitting-room: today the fire that had burned

Shadrach was unlit. The mother sat between her two sons. Mr Chimbley on a hard chair faced the family and withdrew a few sheets of paper from a leather file.

But the lady was the first to speak.

'Let's get this over chop-chop. Alfred's dead and gone, it's time to move on. We all want to know where we're at, so you go ahead, you say your piece, Mr Chimbley.'

He cleared his throat and said: 'The late Mr Alfred Collins, whose name is now being changed to Collins-Yockenthwaite, made his will eighteen days before his death. It has not been altered in any respect. There are two clauses in all. Clause A bequeathes a sum of money not exceeding one million pounds to his widow, and another sum not exceeding one million pounds to his younger son, Davey. Clause B leaves Goose Farm and its outbuildings and land and the residue of his estate to his elder son, George. That concludes his last will and testament.'

Davey broke the silence.

'No, I'm not standing for that!'

His mother screamed at Mr Chimbley: 'Come again, mate – you've got your sums wrong!'

Davey again, on his feet, flushed and furious, gave tongue.

'I'm not accepting one million out of twenty, it's chicken feed, it's sewage. And it's unprofessional conduct, Mr whoever-you-are, you shouldn't have let my father make a nonsense of a will when he was half-dead and out of his mind. I'll report you to the legal authorities – you look out! I'll

get this will rewritten if it's the last thing I do.'
He turned to George. 'Why are you sitting there
so smug? You're not stealing my money, George,
I'm warning you. Why don't you speak up for
fair dealing and fair-dos? You're all right, you
selfish sod, you couldn't care less about your
mother and brother. You won't get away with it,
I'm telling you!'

Mr Chimbley tried to speak, but was shouted
down.

Then George boomed: 'Shut up! Shut up!'
Hermione and Davey were surprised and silenced.
George added: 'Mr Chimbley's got more to say.
Sit down, Davey! Sit and listen!'

Mr Chimbley said: 'Mr Davey is incorrect in
his reference to twenty million pounds. That is
the gross figure, the net amount after the payment
of death duty, forty per cent of the estate which
includes Goose Farm, will be approximately eleven
million pounds.'

Davey shrilled: 'That's a con – nine million
vanishing into thin air? – tell me another,
Chimbley!'

'It is law, not a con, and all three of you will
be fined heavily and even imprisoned if you fail
to pay what is demanded by the Inland Revenue.'

'Well, I'll be getting another solicitor – that's
a fact, too.'

'You are at liberty to do so. But the sum of
eleven million is not twelve million because your
father instructed me to set aside a contingency
fund specifically to pay for a legal defence of his
will against any challenge mounted by one or

more of his heirs. May I also say that the sanity of your father was proven by Doctor Hall in Teasham, Mr Burns, the bank manager of our branch of the NatWest, and two of my colleagues, both solicitors – their names and written statements can be provided. Finally, I should warn Mr Davey that I am always prepared to invoke the laws of libel. Good day.'

Mr Chimblcy stood.

George, also standing, said: 'Please don't go, stay and have a cup of tea.'

The other two did not reinforce the invitation.

'Another time, sir,' Mr Chimbley replied stiffly. 'May I have a word in private as I walk to my car?'

The goodbyes of the mother and the second son were grudging, and Mr Chimbley's were professional. Out of doors he and George made an appointment to meet in Teasham: there were loose ends to be tied, and Mr Burns would be waiting to deal with banking matters and investments.

George said: 'I'm afraid my people were disappointed, and showed it. I must apologise to you. My brother can be excitable and silly. We all have a lot to adjust to.'

'True,' Mr Chimbley replied, but shook George's hand and drove off with a smile.

Indoors, George had to play the part of Saint Sebastian. He was pierced and punctured by the arrows shot at him by his own mother – Davey was absent for some reason. He found her shedding tears of anger against her dead husband, of self-pity, frustrated greed, hatred of Mr Chimbley, and simple rage at the beneficiary who had done so much better than herself and her favourite son.

'How could your father have been so unkind? How could he have done this to me?' she blubbed.

'You weren't very kind to him, Mother.'

'Why do you think you know what that man did to me, or didn't do? He was a weakling, he was pathetic. He was indebted to me, I propped him up, and now he's had his revenge by taking what's rightly mine. And you're not cleverer than me because you're richer, George.'

'Oh Mother!'

'It's cruel to cut out Davey. It's to spite me. Davey's a lovely boy, and he's been hurt by his father since the day he was born. It was always you, George – you stole Davey's birthright, and you've stolen his inheritance. I'd kill your father if I had the chance.'

'Please stop, Mother.'

'Oh no, that's not what I'm going to do. There'll have to be a review of the will – we'll do it together. You're not to run away with your cash.'

'I have no intention of running away.'

'Oh, you're so perfect, George, you make me sick. You're never going to be the head of my family. I'm the head, the brains, I am, and you'll take your orders from me, not from that snivelling lawyer who's not trustworthy. Ask him what he's getting out of Alfred's will!'

She rambled on, and Davey rejoined the party.

'I've found another solicitor to fight our battle,' he said to his mother. 'He's a London man, he recommends legal action, and I've instructed him to go ahead and prepare a case against George.'

'For heaven's sake, Davey!' George exclaimed repressively. 'Have you any idea of the expense you've involved yourself in!'

'You'll be bearing the expense,' Davey retorted. 'I'll win costs and damages, which you'll pay, and justice.'

'Well, you might have thought of asking me for help before being so aggressive.'

'Your help has hindered me always. I'm tired of being patronised by you. Father was a bastard in my opinion, or maybe I'm the bastard, because he and I were poles apart – who was my father, Mother? No, don't answer – I've got no quarrel with you – not yet, anyway – I'm taking my own steps to obtain the money that should be mine, and I need. I'm not a farmhand like you, George.'

And so it went on, staple family fare in the next few days.

Then Hermione and Davey went up to London, leaving a brusque note but no explanation. They returned in a Ferrari two-seater with a supercharged engine.

George was furious, and said: 'What did you buy the car with? The money hasn't been distributed yet, we've got to go to the bank before our accounts are opened. How have you paid for the car?'

'You're paying,' Davey replied.

Hermoine expanded on that answer: 'We've been very naughty, George. We borrowed your passport and wrote a little note to bearer signed with your name. Sorry, dear! We had to pay over the odds for insurance. Anyway, we signed on the dotted line, and you'll get an invoice soon. We can all use the car, can't we?'

On the night before the appointments with Messrs Chimbley and Burns, George proposed a peace treaty or at least an armistice.

What did they want, how much did they want?

Hermione was prepared to step aside in a financial sense if her sons could agree on a settlement. Davey argued for not less than fifty per cent, half the sum George had inherited. George stated his terms.

'In return for doing as Davey wishes, I would have to become the only resident here, Goose Farm would have to be mine alone. I would not be responsible for bills for future life-styles, for day-to-day expenses or extravagance – illness might be an exception to that rule. I would not be liable for your debts, or under any obligation to rush to your rescue. I'm sorry if I sound hard or heartless, but I would need a legally binding document signed by all three of us, making it impossible for either of you or for me to trespass on one another's preserves. What about that?'

Hermione looked at Davey, who said, 'It's a basis, I suppose,' and left the room.

The next day the three of them crushed into the Ferrari and drove into Teasham.

In Mr Chimbley's office George gave the solicitor the gist of the hypothetical deal.

Mr Chimbley showed signs of scepticism, and said: 'Would you be requiring my advice?'

Davey, not George, answered: 'Not at all!'

Mr Chimbley was not discouraged.

'In the circumstances, since Mr Davey would have a vested interest in no spokes being put in his spinning wheel, I believe it is my duty to state the legal implications of the document you, Mr George, have in mind. It could be drafted, such a document, but how binding it would be in a court of law is a moot point.'

'And the fifty-fifty rearrangement?' George inquired.

'That, too, could be legalised, in a manner of speaking. But Mr Davey's share will be minus one million pounds already received.'

'Oh my God,' Davey groaned rudely.

Mr Chimbley cleared his throat and resumed: 'It would be a dereliction of duty not to inform you, Mr George, that in my opinion and the light of my experience I believe you should have at least fifty-one per cent of your father's bequest and Mr Davey no more than forty-nine.'

'Unacceptable,' Davey shouted.

Hermione butted in.

'George, be fair, I do beg you, Davey minds it all so much and you're not a materialistic person, let it be exactly halved. If you can't, or you won't, I don't think I could ever forgive you.'

After a long pause George said: 'Oh hell! Okay.'

The brothers ended up with four and a half million pounds apiece after paying Mr Chimbley's fee and expenses. In a legal sense Goose Farm was split in two, George owning one half and Davey the other. Hermione had no more than her original bequest of a million.

The document establishing this revised form of the estate of Alfred Collins-Yockenthwaite was meant to be irreversible and not open to misinterpretation. But George was already unhappy about it. His generosity had not saved him from being blackmailed by his mother, he was more aware of Davey's ingratitude than of anybody's gratitude, and afraid he had been foolish to yield to the temptation not to pay attention to grubby details.

The preoccupations of the brothers at Goose Farm were different. Here again, they differed expensively. George carried on from where he had left off in South Africa, he tried to make agricultural sense of the farm. He worked long hours in the fields, getting rid of thistles, ploughing and planting. Davey on the other hand did precious little, watched TV, bought things, wasted his pent-up energy, and plotted to do down his brother. He employed a building firm to construct an additional room large enough to hold a full-size billiards table: the first thing George knew of it was the arrival of lorry loads of bricks, steel and concrete, and the second thing was a huge bill for the whole of the cost. Then Davey had the drive tarmacked and gritted; had the house decorated inside and out; and bought literal tons of furniture.

George objected, but Davey made rows that lasted for days and rendered life hardly worth living. George offered to buy his brother out: Davey refused. What was he playing at, George asked, what was his game? Davey said he was after George's half of the property, to buy it for a few thousand pounds, a fraction of its worth.

George began to pine for accommodation not shared physically with his mother and brother. He would prefer anywhere else, house, flat, room, shed. His mother's siding with her younger son against the elder was unfair and nasty, and Davey's hatred and malice, and manic fecklessness, were intolerable. Parties of young men congregated at Goose Farm in the evenings and played snooker into the small hours to win money or lose it. The results were horrible noise, desperate snooker players, drunkenness, fights, injuries, ambulances, policemen, and visits from belligerent parents. Davey was involved in the gambling, although he swore he was not, and his mother believed him; and he would not mend his ways.

Without warning mother and brother went missing. They left no note, they were gone for ten days, during which George agonised over whether or not to call in the police. They might have been dead, although he was more worried about scandal. They returned in high good humour, in the Ferrari, in straw hats bearing the motto, *Vive la France,* and said they had been in Dieppe. Why Dieppe, George wondered. He wondered if there was a casino in Dieppe. Soon afterwards he was contacted by Mr Burns, who broke the rules of confidentiality to warn George that his brother had spent large sums of money on the Continent and could be heading for a financial crisis. George was urged and felt obliged to broach the subject: he received a flea in his ear – Davey told him in barrackroom language to mind his own business.

George wished he could seek advice. He thought of consulting Mr Chimbley, but fear held him back: he was afraid of uncovering a calamity, of having to do dreadful things, of ruination in every sense. He either turned the other cheek or averted his eyes. He tilled the soil in the two paddocks, on the right and the left of the drive to Goose Farm. At the back of his mind lurked the notion that the miasma of money could clear off and he would find himself where he had been at Peak Holding, poor and hungry.

The build-up to the climax disguised itself as a lull. Davey was busy for a change. He drove out in the Ferrari early, missed meals, and was apt to come home late. He was more polite, he laughed more or giggled. The snooker finished at civilised hours or did not occur. Another surprise was that Hermione warned George that she meant to return to South Africa. He was temporarily relieved: if only he could also get rid of his brother he would have Goose Farm to himself, could look for a nice girl to marry, raise a family and live a proper life at last. But he realised he would have no buffer between himself and his brother. He would be cooking for Davey, everything would be worse rather than better. Then he received Mr Chimbley's summons.

He caught the bus into Teasham. In Mr Chimbley's office he was asked if he intended to build houses in one of his paddocks. 'What? No!' he replied, and his heart sank.

Morgan Chimbley said: 'Planning permission to build twenty houses on the western paddock has been applied for by the owner of the land and builders called Weedon and Smith.'

'Oh God!'

'I'm sorry to be the bearer of bad news, Mr George.'

'Is that all?'

'No, sir.'

'What else?'

'Mr Davey's account at the bank is overdrawn.'

'He can't have spent four million pounds.'

'Larger sums can be lost on the spin of a roulette wheel, I understand.'

'There can't be any more folly.'

'The owner of the paddock in question has invested in the project.'

'Is that where the money's gone?'

'No. His money went before he made the investment.'

'What are you suggesting?'

'He's borrowed in order to invest.'

'What could he borrow against?'

'Against the value of Goose Farm, I expect.'

'His half of Goose Farm isn't worth that much.'

'No, sir. Has Mr Davey asked you to invest in his project?'

'No – not a word – nothing.'

'Possibly he has borrowed against the understanding that you would back him with property and cash.'

'I'm not paying. There are limits. He wants the lot. He'll never be satisfied till we're both on the rocks. He's not all there, Mr Chimbley, the money's pushed him over the edge. What am I to do?'

'You'll have to talk to your brother.'

'It won't do any good.'

'You can say no and mean it. You hold the purse strings, after all.'

'I put nothing past him.'

'Are you referring to violence, sir?'

'I could be.'

'Would you like me to be present when you have the talk?'

'You can't live at Goose Farm.'

'Your mother, sir, wouldn't she help you to make him see sense?'

'She's as wrong in the head as he is, she encourages him and blames me.'

'She couldn't find fault with your generosity, Mr George.'

'But where does generosity end and silliness begin? I won't be silly. I can buy a quiet life with money, or I could, if Davey wasn't dead set on stealing my every penny. It's true, Mr

100

Chimbley! Remember what I've said. I'll have another shot at sorting him out. Goodbye.'

George trod the streets of Teasham. He was filled with despondency and dread. He was tempted to take a train to nowhere, and resisted – escapism was not allowed by his character and conscience. The day closed in, dusk fell, and he caught a bus to the stop by The Queen's Head and walked to Goose Farm. The Ferrari was in the yard, Davey was at home. The time was just on seven o'clock.

They met in the sitting-room. Davey shuffled his papers as George walked in. They exchanged hullos.

'Where's Mother?' George asked.

'Upstairs, she wasn't feeling well.'

'I know you're in trouble, Davey – I've been with Mr Chimbley.'

Davey did not respond. He did none of the things George had braced himself for. He did not flare up, hit the roof, cry blue murder, deny anything. He seemed to shrink a bit, sitting on the sofa and gazing at his brother in not too fierce a way.

George resumed: 'You've spent all your money, and borrowed more to invest in building houses down in the paddock. That's right, isn't it?'

Davey's reply seemed to answer another question.

'Bad timing,' he said.

'What?'

'Planning permission's been delayed. It's late. If it had been punctual, if it had come through,

101

my paddock would have been worth fifteen mill at least. You spoke to Mr Chimbley too soon.'

'I'm not a property developer, Davey.'

'No – nor you are – not your fault. You won't lend me the money I owe?'

'How much have you borrowed?'

'Oh I don't know.'

'You do.'

'Okay, three million.'

'When do you have to pay back the loan?'

'Now.'

'Why did you do it?'

'You could afford to lend it to me, George.'

'We both know you'd want the rest, you'd have the last quarter of my remaining capital, you would, Davey, all my four and a half millions, not to speak of my whole inheritance.'

'Sorry,' he said.

'I'm sorry too.'

'Let's go out somewhere for supper.'

'What, Davey? I can't keep up with you.'

'Why don't we bury the hatchet? Money's not worth a fight to the death, is it? Look, Mother didn't want to be disturbed, she's not at all well. We can't do anything for her, and I don't want to cook – do you? I'll give you a meal at The Halfway House – you know, along the straight bit of road where the Ferrari could get some exercise.'

'I don't believe you, Davey.'

'That's the trouble.'

'How are you going to wriggle out of the trap you're in? Not by buying me supper.'

'Oh George, for once, once again, trust me, give me a chance if you won't give me money. I'll survive, I'm not going under, I'm cleverer than you think, honestly! Please, let's try to be friends.'

'No.'

'Please!'

'Oh Davey. What's to be done with you?'

'I'll tell you over supper.'

They left Goose Farm, clambered into the Ferrari, pottered along to the straight road, and accelerated.

At eight-thirty Mr Chimbley was informed of the accident. The two Yockenthwaite brothers had been killed by the crash into a solid oak tree on the side of a road. The cause of the accident was not known, although a possible cause was the discovery of both brothers' hands clamped to the steering wheel. The verdict of the coroner's inquest was death by misadventure.

Some days and nights later Morgan Chimbley reported to Heather at bedtime.

'I've heard from that woman, the mother of the Yockenthwaite boys, Hermione, she calls herself. She's written to tell me she's going back to South Africa to end her days there.'

'Oh how sad, the mother too!'

'She used the word "terminal". If she expires there'll be no living heir to any further disbursement of Yockenthwaite funds.'

'That's a pity, isn't it?'

'Not a pity for us, dear. We could be the heirs of the rest of Shadrach's money.'

'My goodness! Do you mean millions, Morgan?'

'I do.'

'You deserve every penny, but I suppose we mustn't get too excited just yet?'

'Better not.'

'Why did those boys die, Morgan? I know the car hit a tree, but were they drunk or something?'

'I'm afraid one of them was greedy, which is a deadly sin.'

Fifth Chapter of Nine

Ambrose Thwaite and his wife Beatrice were breaking bread in the sun-lounge of their home in Northumberland. It was November and no sun shone. The bread had been baked by Beatrice: it was of a dense and heavy consistency. A third place was set at the breakfast table, but the third pottery cup, saucer and plate had not yet been used. The time was between eight and nine o'clock.

The Thwaites' dwelling crouched alone on a cliff. The sea was not far distant, the nearest village was Long Bolwark, and the town of Ambly was twenty-five miles away. The prevailing wind was from the north, and a little shelter was provided by a clump of bending evergreens. The bungalow had a roof of heavy stone slabs which had just about withstood numberless gales and storms. It had a shed attached, a so-called studio, literally tethered by a chain to the brickwork of the bungalow.

The externals of The Pottery, the name of the property, told a tale of either poverty or infirmity. A feeble fence of driftwood and rusty wire netting surrounded it. In 'gardens' front and back overgrown greenery, weeds and a clothes line fought for space. The exterior woodwork of the studio was blanched, and the salt in the air had long ago stripped the paint from all painted surfaces. A dilapidated wooden garage housed an ancient Rover. A grassy track led to and from the main road.

The interior of The Pottery, in estate agents' terms, was two recep, two bed, bathroom, kitchen and cloakroom. The studio could be 'extra accommodation'. Measurements in general were on the skimpy side. On the other hand, the dwelling was picturesque, in a romantic location, had sea views, was within easy reach of a sandy beach, and ready for modernisation. It was connected to telephone, electricity supply, public water, and its septic tank was emptied regularly.

As a home, The Pottery was cosy in a fashion. Its interior was a demonstration of the Arts and Crafts movement in action. No space on floor or walls was without an item of the Thwaite range of artefacts, earth-coloured objects thrown on the potter's wheel, wood carvings, pokerwork, crocheted rugs, rag rugs, samplers, paintings in watercolour and crayon, woodcuts and linocuts, all framed decoratively. The various impressions on a stranger, in the unlikely event of a stranger visiting, would have been that The Pottery was amusing and delightful, or a work of art fit to be exhibited in the Tate Gallery.

The owners claimed to be – or would have claimed if challenged – simple folk in spite of their middle class origins: crafts people, modest artists, parents devoted to their only child, and a soul brother and a soul sister of the downtrodden masses. They were polite and kindly. They were Good Samaritans in principle. But they dropped hints to those who had eyes to see and ears to hear that they were proud of their cleverness, integrity, and left-wing inclinations.

They looked alike, as couples married for a long time often do. They might have been brother and sister, but not incestuous ones. They were both slim, and still quick on their feet. He was sixty-five, she was sixty-seven. They had met at an Adult Education Art Class in Islington, and plighted their troth in a civil ceremony thirty-six years ago. They had much in common, their interest in handicrafts and complementary skills, their social consciences, hatred of the modern urban world, idealism combined with agnosticism verging on atheism, and shy reclusiveness. He had worked in a printing business, she had looked after her parents. He had savings, she had inherited capital. For each of them, their marriage made sense. Love must have come into it, but was not a top priority.

They were kindred spirits or – politically – comrades. They were sprites or elves. They were asexual to the point of sexlessness. He had a wedge-like face and sharp nose, she had freckles and wore her hair in a kind of bun. Time did not damage or change them physically or mentally. They were sure of themselves, and that they were right.

But the ointment that does not have a fly in it is a rarity.

The Thwaites shared a bed, but an exception or two proved their rule that for them it was to sleep in. They talked and worked together, and for a decade that was roughly that. Beatrice's pregnancy was embarrassing. They made the best of what they both regarded as a bad job. A daughter was born in due course, and they supposed, they agreed, that they were lucky. They called her Candida, and twenty-six years later the consequence was the third place laid in the sunless sun lounge of The Pottery. Candida was as usual late for breakfast.

Ambrose and Beatrice had stood up pretty well to her infancy. They managed her childhood neatly, since they kept her interference with their lives to a minimum. They took turns to be distracted by her. They put her to bed early and did not allow her out of her bedroom until they were prepared. They found an infant school for her, then the other schools she needed within walking or bicycling distance. She was able to win herself a place in a university several hundred miles from The Pottery, where she could board in a hall of residence: they congratulated her with feeling.

Unfortunately for the elder Thwaites university vacations were long and Candida was controversial. Her brain worked too well: she had deduced that she was an unwanted child and resented it. She was never afraid of her parents, and now in her spotty youth and early womanhood she thought she saw through them, and was uncooperative, and obstinate. She was lumpish, lay about reading, got through homework too quickly, and was frightfully hungry. And she was forming opinions of her own and taking issue with the dogma of her parents. She refused to admire their craftsmanship, she said her father's pots were ugly and her mother's samplers were pointless. She was nasty about The Pottery, called it neolithic, and urged disposal and a move down to London. She even wanted to go to church – Ambrose had to drive her in the Rover. She complained about her pocket money, and said she was mis to have to live with misers.

It was a relief when Candida won a scholarship to an American seat of learning, California Knowledge Inc. She stayed in the USA for two years: but she came home. She had been at home for several weeks before the particular day in November on which she was an hour and a half late for breakfast.

Ambrose had lost patience and gone across to the studio. Beatrice was a determined little person; but her fleshy daughter with the big bony head, the thatch of mousy hair and alarming features, critical eyes, aggressive nose, loose lips and savage teeth, seemed to fuse her nervous system. She kept on going into the kitchen to re-boil the kettle for Candida's coffee and re-heat the oil in the frying pan for Candida's egg. Should she make the toast yet, she asked herself. Where was the newspaper? The Times, yesterday's edition, was brought to them by Farmer Wilcough on his way to feed his bullocks or sheep in the top steading; but Beatrice worried it might not arrive in time to suit Candida. At last she heard a door slam upstairs and the noises-off of ablutions. And luckily *The Times* was pushed through the letter box that squeaked.

The ritual of Candida's breakfast proceeded. She ignored her mother's efforts to converse. She munched and read the paper. When she said something, she did not attend to her mother's rejoinder. She opened the paper violently and uttered obscure curses. At some point her jaws ceased to masticate, she was reading as if with close interest.

Then she said: 'Fetch Daddy, will you?'

Beatrice obeyed. She ran across to the studio and interrupted the throwing of a pot.

Ambrose exclaimed: 'Drat!'

On the way back to the bungalow he asked: 'What's she like today?'

'Grumpy,' Beatrice replied.

'Why does she want me?'

'Something in the paper…'

In the kitchen he addressed Candida with false enthusiasm: 'Good morning, dear! I hope you're well?'

Candida spoke: 'Listen!' She then read aloud another of Mr Morgan Chimbley's advertisements. At the end she asked her father: 'Are you a Yockenthwaite?'

'Well, as a matter of fact I suppose I am, although I'd quite forgotten. My grandfather – or was it my great grandfather? – abbreviated our name to Thwaite. But we knew no Yockenthwaites. The fuller name was not bandied about in our hearing. There might have been something disreputable about the people bearing it.'

'You must answer the ad all the same.'

'Oh no, dear. I couldn't be bothered. There's always a catch in those things. It's probably advertising insurance or a gold mine.'

Beatrice sniggered scornfully at the mention of gold.

Candida frowned and said: 'This ad's put in by a solicitor. It's not commercial, it could be the opposite of an appeal for money. You don't have to be caught, Daddy, you're a grown man and could say no.'

'We don't need money, dear.'

Beatrice chimed in: 'We're not money people, Candida.'

'Oh God!' Candida was cross. 'You choose to live like paupers – more fool you, I say – but you've no right to choose to leave me penniless. I reject your attitude to money. If you won't answer this ad, I will, I can say I'm as much a Yockenthwaite as you are. And if there's money in it, I won't give you a penny.'

'Please calm down, dear.'

'I will not!'

'Do eat your breakfast, Candida.'

'No, I won't. I'm going for a walk, and I'll ring Mr Chimbley when I come back if you haven't.'

Candida flung out of the house, and walked for miles. She walked not for pleasure but to subdue her rage against her parents, her unappealing looks, her sex-starvation, her uncertain future and a cruel world. She was back at The Pottery for a lunch of lettuce leaves, goat's cheese, more homemade bread, and baked apples and custard.

Ambrose had rung Mr Chimbley. He had almost eaten his hat. He had caved in to Candida, agreed to find his way to Teasham, take a DNA test, and then to hear whatever it was that the solicitor wished to say. He would have to stay the night in a bed and breakfast place. Beatrice had decided not to accompany him, she felt unequal to a wild goose chase, and she had work to do on a piece of pokerwork.

Candida put her foot down: her parents had to stop being hopeless. She would drive her father in the old Rover and nanny him throughout. Actually she was more a boss than a nanny, but Ambrose did not complain. They found the surgery in Teasham largely by argument, and a spot of blood was taken. They ate a not very high tea in a café, and stayed in separate rooms in a B&B. The next morning they passed the time with difficulty until they were due in Mr Chimbley's office. There, Ambrose was told that he had inherited ten million pounds.

He covered his face with his hands and rocked back and forwards on his chair as if in pain. Candida jumped half out of her chair, uttering a hoarse cry of triumph, and punching the air with a closed fist. The solicitor held up his hand, a gesture that combined with the expression on his face and conveyed the message, 'Desist, if you please!'

Order was restored. Ambrose mopped his eyes and forehead with a tissue, then had a fit of sneezing. Candida hit her father on the back several times, an ambiguous treatment for whatever afflicted him. Mr Chimbley was running through his rigmarole in such situations, a reference or two to Shadrach, and the new relationship between Ambrose and the Commissioners of Inland Revenue. He also mentioned Goose Farm, a small rural estate, the traditional seat of the Yockenthwaite family, which his firm, Chimbley Chimbley and Davis, had maintained off and on for several years.

It was nearly lunchtime. Either because Candida was hungry, or because Ambrose was in a state of bewilderment, further discussion was postponed until the afternoon. The two Thwaites were ushered out of the solicitor's premises, and Candida guided her father towards and into an Italian restaurant, Marco's, near their B&B.

Ambrose came to his senses, or some of them, after Candida had spoken to a waiter.

'Did I hear you say "champagne", dear?' he inquired.

'You did. We're celebrating. I noticed this restaurant yesterday evening and promised myself a meal here if we should hit the jackpot today. We'll have a damn good lunch, Daddy, and drink to our relation, Shadrach. Yes, we will – don't make difficulties! You're a multimillionaire, like it or not. Anyway, I like it, and I'm going to spend a chunk of your money.'

'Oh heavens! Oh no! What is this place?'

'It's an Italian eatery, it's expensive, and we're in Teasham, Daddy, and you can afford it.'

'I don't feel comfortable in such places, Candida. I haven't been in a restaurant for many years. I think we should be getting home.'

'Nonsense, Daddy! We're staying another night in Teasham, we'll have to look over Goose Farm tomorrow. This afternoon we're back with Mr Chimbley, our solicitor, God bless his cotton socks! And I'll book a couple of nice rooms in that hotel we passed, The Anchor. You'll sleep in a civilised joint tonight. Put that in your pipe!'

'Candida ... I can't get used to your language, Candida. I'm afraid we misunderstand each other. I can't approve of extravagance. Shadrach's left us money, but I'm not going to change my spots. I'm grateful to our relative, however he acquired so much money, and I shall use it wisely, I hope, but please remember that your dear mother and I have our values and our principles.'

The waiter appeared with a bottle of champagne and champagne glasses. He opened the bottle with a pop and was about to serve the gentleman and his young companion. Candida had cracked a joke or two with the waiter.

Ambrose said to him: 'Not for me, thank you.'

Candida protested.

'Oh come on, Daddy, this is a once in a lifetime thing, don't be a party-pooper!'

114

'White wine doesn't agree with me, it's too acid.'

'One glass, one sip, won't do you any harm. If you're going to be a mule, I'll have to drink the whole bottle.'

'Pour the wine,' Ambrose said to the man who was waiting in every sense.

Candida was lifting her glass.

She said: 'Let's drink to better times.'

'Oh I don't think I can do that – it would be ungrateful – I've had such a happy life – and couldn't ask for anything better.'

'You're out of date, Daddy. Your life's changed. I'll give you another toast: let's keep our minds open and our hearts ready to adjust. Clink glasses?'

They did so. They ordered food, a salad for Ambrose, meat for Candida, then cheddar cheese for him and a Black Forest gateau for her.

Towards the end of the meal he said: 'I ought to ring your mother.'

'Go ahead,' she replied.

'I dread it – she'll take the news so hard.'

Candida roared with laughter.

'It's not funny, dear,' he said. 'We're so settled in our quiet ways ... Perhaps you don't have much respect for craftwork ... We're not worldly or ambitious. You should see what an upheaval it will be for us to approve of what we've always been against, excessive wealth, materialism. How are we to be capitalists?'

'Sorry, Daddy. The joke is that you respond to a windfall of ten cool millions as if it were a death in the family. People would think you mad if they could hear you. You'll have to adjust a bit more quickly than you are adjusting to your new status.'

'You make me feel I'm having a nightmare when you talk to me like that.'

'Well, it's not a nightmare. You've been saved by the bell – which is another phrase you won't understand. But listen, listen! You and Mother are growing old, one of you is going to fall by the wayside – no, you can't depend on dying hand-in-hand at the same time – and what then? You couldn't manage on your own in The Pottery, Mother certainly couldn't, and I'm not offering my services. Without this money you've been left, you'll find your quiet way, clinging to a clifftop by your fingernails, is impractical, beyond your strength, and you'll be removed from your home, you'll be at the tender mercy of the Welfare State, the clapped-out social services and the fever pits of the NHS.'

'You're saying horrible things, Candida.'

'I'm telling you the truth, which gets less idealistic, unreal, and twee the more you look at it. Who'll cook and keep house for you when you're a widower, who'll shop and drive Mother about when she's a widow? Who'll keep you company? You'll need to pay for help, you'll certainly need more money than you had yesterday, you might need all the money you've inherited today. You and mother are all for independence and the dignity of the individual. Old age isn't independent, and the more dignified you want it to be the more it costs.'

'I'm greatly saddened by the way you talk, dear.'

'Well, cheer up, Daddy, and eat your lettuce.'

He did as he was told, at least he picked at the food, while he spoke of the humanitarian beliefs he and his wife had embraced, that man was born free, and we were all equal, that the love of money was the root of all evil, and that it was better to dig your garden in a peaceful place than to jostle and elbow other people aside in the rat race.

'Have another glass of champagne,' Candida said.

'No, thank you. Water, please.' Ambrose resumed: 'Luxury is sinfulness in our eyes. We didn't want it, we hated it, our ethic is connected with honest work and simplicity. Maybe modern people would think us peculiar to spurn what they would call luck, but there it is. We'll have to give the money away.'

'Beg pardon, Daddy?'

'I think you heard me.'

'Give it to whom?'

'Deserving causes.'

'You won't have to give it to the government, the government's taking forty per cent of it.'

'There are starving people in Africa.'

'Africa is much richer than you are. North Africa has oil, and South Africa's made of gold and diamonds, but Africa doesn't help Africans. Africa waits for philanthropists with soft hearts and soft heads like you to feed the Africans who support crooked politicians and warmongers and

117

find they're homeless and hungry and being killed in droves.'

'Oh your cynicism, Candida – where did you learn to be so cynical – not from your mother or me!'

'I won't let you throw away money that people have earned with great difficulty somewhere. You must take money more seriously. I'm serious, Daddy. This money you've been left is silly money, money for jam, an exceptional punt, but that doesn't mean it can be treated in a silly way. I'm sorry to have to tell you that you've fallen into the first trap set for rich people, you're thinking money grows on trees. Remember the sweat on the brows and the strains on the strong hearts of the people who made ten million pounds!'

'Why do you think you know so much about riches? It can't be from experience.'

'I have degrees in economics and in history. You and Mother have never given me credit for my academic career. You were never interested in me. That's water under the bridge. Who cares? But, by God, Daddy, I'm not letting you put your airy-fairyness ahead of my interest in this money that's dropped into your lap and mine – mine by birthright. Whatever it does to you and for you and Mother, for me it's a chance to buy a good life or a bad one, to escape from The Pottery, and to beg you to heed me and what I'm trying to din into you. Don't you see?'

Ambrose pondered before replying: 'All I see is that within an hour or two of hearing how rich I am you and I have quarrelled.'

'There's no quarrel.'

'By my standards, there is. I'll leave you now, Candida. I'd like to lie down for a little while before I speak to your mother.'

She escorted him to The Anchor Hotel, and accompanied him to a bedroom. She fetched his luggage from the Rover and delivered it to the hotel, along with her own rucksack. She passed the afternoon looking at clothes she intended to buy as soon as possible. Ambrose appeared at teatime, she was waiting for him at a table for two in the hotel lounge. He was calm and benevolent, and gave her a message.

'Your mother sends you her love. She and I are sorry that you feel we neglected you, and we're hoping to repair damage that was inadvertently done. She was startled by the legacy, but we have solved the problem to our satisfaction. We would like to give the larger part to you, Candida. The legal paperwork can be planned and possibly completed tomorrow.'

She thanked him. She poured the tea and he drank it. They talked of the old days, he did most of it.

Then he said: 'I must admit that I feel quite exhausted, and will return to my room, where I understand a sandwich can be brought to me later in the evening. Thank you for running errands. Good night – until breakfast tomorrow morning!'

They were back in Mr Chimbley's office at nine o'clock the next day.

The division of the spoils was disillusioning

119

for Ambrose. He began by saying that, after further consultation with his dear wife, he had decided to keep ten thousand pounds of his inheritance for use on a rainy day, and was surprised to be shouted down by his daughter and solicitor in unison. They told him, respectively, that ten grand was child's play, and that he was under-estimating the cost of inevitable contingencies. Candida added for good measure: 'You can't afford to be a miser now!' And Mr Chimbley suggested that five hundred thousand pounds should be retained by Mr and Mrs Thwaite, who could of course redirect any residue by means of a will and testament.

Ambrose bowed his head, agreed as if under torture to the half-million, but said Beatrice would be sure to give it to her African orphans or Indian street-children.

He cheered up when he was informed that his bequest to Candida would not be ten million pounds or thereabouts, but, after tax, legal fees and his retention of a portion, only between four and five million. He apologised to his daughter, but could not completely hide his relief that she was not going to be quite so wealthy as he had feared. Mr Chimbley drew attention to schemes that could rescue money from the clutches of the taxman, but Ambrose would have none of that. 'We are happy to pay for the privilege of living in our beautiful country,' he said.

He then asked to be shown the way to the cloakroom. A secretary appeared and received instructions about the preparation of Mr Thwaite's will. Candida told Mr Chimbley not to bother her father about Goose Farm: 'Keep on maintaining the property, I'll deal with it in due course.' She also talked to Mr Burns on the telephone and ordered cheque books and so on: she would bring her father into the bank in a few hours – they would both sign the necessary documents.

Elevenses were served in Mr Chimbley's office. The will was signed and witnessed. Candida helped her father back to the hotel, where he rested until they met for lunch – she ate it, he toyed with another salad; and after a half-hour session in the NatWest with Mr Burns, they set off for Norfolk.

Ambrose was confused. He fretted about how much money he had in his bank account, and more so about how much he was giving away.

Yet at another moment he said: 'To think you have to go through all that rigmarole if you want to give your daughter more pocket money – what is this world of ours coming to!'

She corrected him: 'It's not pocket money, Daddy,' and added under her breath: 'and if it is it won't stay in my pocket for long.'

Twelve months passed. Ambrose and Beatrice had aged more in one year than they had in thirty. They were not so healthy as they had been. They now took pills for blood pressure, cholesterol, digestion, pain in their hips and knees, and sleeping. Their way of life was restricted.

121

They grew less food in their garden, and motored into Ambly once a week, to the supermarket there, partly to buy supplies for their freezer – they ate frozen meals. The Rover sometimes let them down, they ordered taxis with regret – they had to have taxis for night drives to the doctor's surgery in winter, Ambrose's eyesight was not equal to driving in the dark. Their arts and crafts suffered. Ambrose made plates and tiles instead of throwing pots, Beatrice had to stop doing needlework and carving with sharp tools, she concentrated on her watercolours. They exhibited at Gift Fairs less frequently, and their artefacts crowded onto shelves and into bulging cupboards.

The trouble was money. They did not say so, they would not stoop to think so; but the windfall had upset their apple cart. It had had an evil effect, though not through love of it, rather the opposite. They tried to be logical. They did not lose sight of what they had lived for, and on, in the good old days before they were rich. Ambrose had inherited a capital sum from an aunt, twenty-five thousand pounds, and Beatrice had private means when they married, she was the beneficiary of a trust fund set up by her grandfather, she received an income of three hundred pounds a year. With sales of their works they had managed to support their three selves, counting their daughter, on their slender income; but, strictly speaking, they were not living from hand to mouth, like real workers, like that class of people they identified with, they had been reliant on unearned money, on capital, they had been capitalists without knowing it, and Shadrach's money had not changed their economic status except in size and value.

Why, then, had they been knocked sideways?

Reason told them they were being unreasonable. But their consciences told them a different story. They suspected that Candida had seen through their pretensions that they were working-class or classless, not grinding the faces of the poor, suspended above and beyond the harsher realities of economics, wages, competition. They feared they had been hypocrites; and belonged in the category of the people they despised, the liars and frauds; and Candida was as right as they had been wrong.

The five hundred thousand pounds in their bank was a heavy burden on their shoulders. They were ashamed to spend it, they felt foolish not to do so. Clifftop residences beside the sea, old cars, taxis, shop vegetables, were costing more money than they had once thought they would. They delved into their half-million. A crisis had been predicted, and occurred. Beatrice was immobilised by arthritis in her hip, Ambrose could not lift her, they were caught out by calls of nature, cooking, eating, and the rest of it. The NHS offered a free operation in eight months. The same operation by a surgeon who said he charged eight thousand pounds was available in ten days. They had to agree to go private, there seemed no other option. The total price they paid was between eight and ten thousand pounds, a fraction of their capital; the operation was successful, but it had the effect of a slow poison of their moral constitutions.

Ambrose faced a fact or two, if only out of the corner of his eye. They should not live any longer in The Pottery. He persuaded Beatrice that the alternatives to not moving house were unthinkable, ambulances were fifteen miles distant, their neighbours, the farmer and his wife called Wilcough, not near enough for comfort. There was a house in Ambly they both liked, not too big, pretty, and for sale. The asking price was four hundred and fifty thousand pounds.

It was a great shock to the Thwaites, another shock. They had expected it to cost in the region of fifty thousand, and an estate agent had valued The Pottery at a fraction of the same sum. The modern world was madder than they had thought it, and beyond their means.

They did not blame Candida. They never had, blame was not part of their humanism. But when they discussed their discovery that they were more or less imprisoned in their Pottery, and could not afford to live where they pleased elsewhere, the topic of their daughter cropped up more often than it had in the days of their satisfaction with their lot.

'Do you think she ever remembers us?' Beatrice would ask Ambrose as they sat by the low fire in their sitting-room in winter, while the wind encircled their home and rain drummed on the windowpanes.

'I expect she does, dear,' Ambrose replied, holding out his thin veiny hands to the flame.

Beatrice was also inclined to ask: 'I do so hope she's spent a little of all that money on our causes. We often talked to her about the good people trying to alleviate the suffering all over the world.'

Ambrose's answers were interrogative.

'Is she generous? What do you think?'

Beatrice called herself 'critical' sometimes, after she had ventured to say that Candida was not quite the child they had both wished for.

'I suppose you and I were too wrapped up in each other, she was jealous of our relationship, and that was why we could never be friends.'

'Oh well,' Ambrose spoke philosophically, 'we fostered her, we were like foster parents, that's how to look at it, and as soon as she could she left us to sink or swim on her own – but I hope not to sink.'

Time passed not as it had, in a creative rush, but apprehensively, because they feared to look ahead. The long winter after Shadrach had disturbed the even tenor of their lives was survived, and spring yielded to summer and its occasionally brighter days. In the afternoon of one of those days the Thwaites were sitting on the wooden seat out of the prevailing wind and in the sunshine from the west. They wore interchangeable clothes and their cotton hats stained by years of exposure to the weather. The scene was exceptionally peaceful, or had been until an engine was audible. A white vehicle was coming up the track across the field, their 'drive', a large vehicle, actually a car, which stopped near The Pottery. It was a limousine, a Rolls-Royce, an 'open' version, with its soft hood down and two people in the front seats.

The Thwaites were on their feet, and saw the driver, a young blonde woman, step out of the car on her side, while a sun-tanned black-haired smallish man stepped out on the other.

The woman called out to them, 'Hullo!' She approached laughing, and said, 'I'm glad to see you don't recognise me.'

Ambrose spoke to Beatrice: 'It's Candida,' and Beatrice denied it.

The woman reached out a hand – no kisses – and her father took it, saying, 'Oh my goodness! Oh my dear!'

'Hullo, Mother.'

Beatrice replied: 'I'm dreaming.'

'Mother, meet my fiancé, Marko – I bought him in Brazil.'

Candida laughed with reminiscent loud laughter, and Marko giggled showing large white teeth.

'I've been wanting to surprise you,' Candida said. 'What do you make of the transformation?'

She assumed coquettish attitudes and continued: 'Spotlight on goldilocks and the body beautiful, with a little help from the surgeon's knife, nose-job, screwed-in teeth, pumped-up breasts and buttocks – not the person you gave birth to, Mother, thanks be to Shadrach Yockenthwaite!'

Beatrice slumped back on to the seat, produced a handkerchief and dabbed her face. Ambrose suggested they should all sit down and indicated other chairs for Marko to pull up.

'Would you like a cup of tea, Candida?' he asked.

'Not much – we've had a vinous lunch – cooking brandy's more to Marko's taste.'

'Oh – well – shall I look for brandy? I don't think we have any.'

'Sit down, Daddy – I was joking. What about my car? Not what you're used to – not many white Rollers come your way. Another thing of beauty, what?'

The Thwaites were reduced to silence by her brashness. When she had rattled on, boasting, laughing at her bad jokes, and stopped to draw breath, Beatrice queried in a feeble little voice: 'Where have you been, dear?'

'Round the world and back again, living a life of leisure, or should I say the life of Riley?'

'No husband yet?'

'Not likely – too expensive a luxury even for me. I prefer slaves.' She gestured at Marko, and said to her parents: 'He doesn't understand English, but he understands enough of what interests me. Sorry, Mother, I'm sure I'm disappointing you again, but no matter – I won't be staying long.'

'What's happened to all that money?'

'Wasted, you would say. I'd say it's made a woman of me, a woman with confidence, and experience galore – well spent, in other words.'

Ambrose ventured to ask: 'We have hoped, Candida, that you would remember the people who are less lucky than we've been and you are.'

'Frankly, I've done my level best to forget a lot of them, the unwashed and undeserving, with their eyes fixed on money for nothing.'

'We tried to bring you up to pity the poor.'

'Come on, Dad! Wake up, Rip van Winkle! Nobody's poor in this country – socialists may tell us people are starving – but people here have money to burn compared with poor people in some other countries – our poor have opted to be irresponsible and pitied. Anyway – I won't be bullied by do-gooders and bleeding hearts.'

Beatrice cried into her handkerchief. Candida rebuked her, 'Oh Mother, spare us!' Ambrose put an arm round his wife's bowed shoulders.

'You speak very harshly, Candida,' he said.

She replied: 'Sorry, Daddy. Fact is, I always thought a spade was a bloody shovel, but I never dared to say so, until now. Your pseudo politics and pseudo religion aren't my cup of tea. I don't believe in saving the lives of murderers and stupid people. There are too many of us – at least fifty per cent have to go to heaven or hell – and they will, nature will see to it – disease or atom bombs, not humanitarian optimists, may really turn this planet into a new Jerusalem. That's my opinion. I'm eating, drinking and trying to be merry. Cheer up, Mother!

'We've failed,' Beatrice whimpered. 'We failed you.'

'Nonsense! Nobody's failed. Thanks to you, I've succeeded – you pointed out the direction I was not to take. Before I hit the trail, how are you both?'

128

Ambrose said: 'We could be worse.'

'Good. I'll be going now.'

Beatrice spoke again.

'Don't go, dear, please, not yet!'

'What's the point? We have nothing in common. We have nothing to talk about. Marko, stir your stumps!'

She and the little man went through the motions of laughter at her joke.

They all stood.

'But where are you going?' Beatrice wailed.

'Over your horizon, into the wild blue yonder. Goodbye, Mother. Goodbye, Daddy, God bless!'

The Thwaites stood together holding hands. Candida and Marko climbed into the Rolls. She drove it in a wide circle and waved as she passed by. The sun was setting, and Ambrose and Beatrice hobbled into The Pottery.

They got through the summer and autumn, and the winter began; but the end was not far ahead. One stormy night Beatrice fell ill. Ambrose tried to ring for an ambulance, the line was dead. He tried to start the Rover, the battery was flat. He set off for Wilcoughs' farm, tripped when crossing a stile, and lay there in the gale and the sheets of rain. Ten days later the double funeral occurred.

Morgan Chimbley felt that he owed it to the family to be there, notwithstanding the distance. He had organised the service in the church at Long Bolwark, although he had a suspicion that the Thwaites were atheists. It was a blustery day, the mourners were few in number, and he caught a chill which developed into a fever. During his convalescence at home he often spoke of the eccentric Thwaites, Ambrose and Beatrice in particular, who had been so unappreciative of their great good fortune. Heather often shook her head disbelievingly when he described the ramshackle shack in which the rich pair had ended their days.

Some months after Morgan had recovered his health and returned to work he reverted to the subject. Again, it was at bedtime, when the Chimbleys were apt to speak from their hearts, or he was anyway.

'Do you recall that I told you the Thwaites had only spent very little of the five hundred thousand pounds of Shadrach's money they had agreed under pressure to accept? Do you remember, Heather?'

'Of course I do, dear,' Heather replied. 'It was unforgettable, and I'm always interested in your little confidences.'

'Thank you, Heather. Now, my problem is that Candida Thwaite should receive that residual money, and I have no way of passing it over to her. I do not know her surname for certain. I have no forwarding address, she removed all her funds from the NatWest long ago, and I have drawn a blank with four advertisements inserted in The Times. My colleagues and Mr Burns are of one mind, that the money should not be left "lying about", in Mr Burns' graphic phrase. We suspect that the young lady might have come to grief, she seemed to be headstrong when I made

130

her acquaintance. I'm wondering what's to be done.'

'You always know better than anyone else, dear.'

'That may be so. All the same, would you like to make a suggestion?'

'Why not keep the money?'

'Very wise. Why not? We could invest it, and repay, of course, should Candida lodge a claim – repay it without any capital gain we might have achieved in the meanwhile.'

'We need to change our car, Morgan.'

'Ah yes.'

Sixth Chapter of Nine

Morgan Chimbley had to work harder for his pickings from the next slice of Shadrach's millions.

His advertisement was answered by a German. The letter was written in German. It was signed Ernst Kuchenmacher: the surname was suspicious, 'cakemaker' was unlikely in any language. The writer claimed to be a Yockenthwaite. He stated that his great-grandfather had been an uncle of Shadrach. Owing to marriages, step-relationships, wars and so on, the writer's father had exchanged his English name for a German one. His late father had been Willibrand Kuchenmacher, and he himself was Ernst; but, if money might be on the table, he was ready and willing to reconsider his nationality and his name.

Verification of these statements took Morgan Chimbley some time – lawyer's time, as they say. He had to have Herr Kuchenmacher's missives translated into English, and his own letters translated into German. At length he was sufficiently satisfied to summon the claimant and authorise a DNA test: it was positive. He gave ten million pounds to the new heir of the Yockenthwaite estate – the sum had materialised from a bank in Monte Carlo.

It was a fortune – more accurately, another fortune. Ernst was already a rich man. He had made a killing not in cakes but in pigs. The ten millions were a good example of coals to Newcastle. He was getting on in years, sixtyish, and not in need of more money.

He was a widower. He had married late, and fathered one child, a daughter, whose mother died giving birth to her. The little girl was called Barbara, and she filled the void left in the heart of Ernst Kuchenmacher by the demise of his Emmy, who had been so cosy and such a tasty cook. He doted on Barbara. He might be hard on his pigs and a tough businessman, but he was soft on Barbara, he was sentimental about her, his eyes filled with tears of adoration when he looked at her, and he spoke her name in a silly maudlin way, 'Baaarbra'.

She was eleven when Ernst inherited from Shadrach. She was a beautiful girl with a romantic disposition, she read poetry and books about love, and was spoilt by her father.

She heard about the inheritance and asked, 'Can I have it?'

He laughed and answered, 'I am leaving you more than ten million in my will, dumpling.' She had sat on his knee when she was a baby and learnt how to flirt. She sat on his knee now in a knowing way, threw her arms round his neck and kissed his big red cheeks and sweaty forehead. Sometimes he kissed her goodnight on the lips: she was aware that it was a treat for him, and she allowed it when she wanted a favour in exchange.

What was she, what happened inside her precociously female figure? She was well aware of her power to charm and influence. She had dreams of beautiful dominating men, and how happy they could make her. The danger hovering over her golden head was that her aspirations clashed with her need to get her own way, and her better self was no match for her impatience and moods of discontent.

She had never known her mother, and not missed her much – she liked to have her father to herself. But not long after Shadrach had smiled on the Kuchenmachers, they were frowned upon. Ernst was unwell. He had a disease from which he could not recover. He made dispositions for his 'dumpling's' future, and arranged his funeral. He also decided that his daughter should be Yockenthwaite rather than Kuchenmacher. It was as Barbara Yockenthwaite, seductively veiled and on the arms of Morgan Chimbley, that she buried Ernest, formerly Ernst, in Teasham church.

She was sixteen. She had a house in Munich and Goose Farm, and she was in charge of a number of people appointed by her father: an English governess and duenna, a middle-aged spinster called Dorothy Wilson, who was installed at Goose Farm; English and German solicitors; doctors waiting in the wings to dole out contraceptives etcetera; and a number of trusty servants and employees. The illness of her father had restrained her and discouraged suitors. But when her period of mourning was over and done with, she returned to Germany and her

German school, where Dorothy could not watch over her.

She was courted by her schoolfellows, and attacked by the jealous cats. She came home to do her homework either with lips swollen by kissing or with her cheeks scratched by female fingernails, occasionally both. She was not exactly fickle or promiscuous, she was looking for a replacement of the man who had adored her. She did not look too far. She retreated into the fastness of her wealth and was called a lesbian by the bad boys.

At seventeen she completed a stage of her German education. She was fluent in English, and spoke it with a pretty accent. At a school concert in honour of the pupils who were leaving, she had to recite a poem in English, Shakespeare's sonnet beginning, *Shall I compare thee to a summer's day?* She stood up in gown and mortarboard, looking very like the summer's day, spoke the lines bewitchingly, then had to approach the guest of honour, a film star from France, Gerard Bollini, who was to give her a copy of the Bible in English.

She approached him and lowered her eyes because he stared so. She took the book, and he gripped her shoulders in his hands, pulled her towards himself, kissed her on both cheeks, and said into her ear: 'Wait for me afterwards.' Her blush deepened. She returned to her seat and felt dazzled as if by beams from his dark eyes under strong black eyebrows. She grew hot all over. He had laddish looks but must have been in his thirties. She obeyed him – he seemed to have stolen her power of independent thought. She lingered until the hall was empty.

He entered from a side door, not from where she expected, and was again holding her before she had time or the presence of mind to step back.

'I love you,' he was saying, 'I want to make love to you. Where can we go? Tell me, tell me!'

She did not know what to do or say. He was pushing, pulling and half-lifting her towards the door he had come through. They were in a passage to an exit from the building. He was talking to and kissing her and doing things to her under her skirt, and she was too weak and bewildered to push him off. And then he turned her round and bent her over and the deed was done. He had called her rude names in French, now she was his 'ange'. He had an official function to attend elsewhere, but said he adored her, and left her to clean up the mess.

In the ensuing days, she ceased to be amazed, she revised her ideas of men, but clung to her ideals in respect of love, and hoped and prayed that Gerard Bollini would keep his word and seek her out.

For a month or so he did not keep it. She agreed to go to Goose Farm with Dorothy Wilson. She felt wronged, also that she had every right to be angry because she was so rich, probably richer than he was, and should and would not be treated as if she were a nobody and a convenience. She paid a visit to one of her doctors and made sure that she was not pregnant with the baby of that rat, Gerard.

He turned up at Goose Farm. He was handsome and charming, bowled over Dorothy and the female members of Barbara's staff; but he did not get what he was there for. He was now the bewildered one. He was amazed. He was not used to rejection. He insisted, pleaded, threatened, begged. She was adamant. She refused to be alone with him. She rebuffed his arguments with one of her own: 'You're not my husband.' He laughed at her, called her a baby, did not know what to do, was short of time, explained that he lived in a rush and was getting tired of waiting for her to let them be happy. Nearly the end of their story was that he proposed marriage, rushed her to a Register Office and straight back to bed.

Their marriage did not suit her at all. They lived in suitcases. He swanked about his income – he should have been considering her capital. He flirted, which was her prerogative. He acted on the premise that he merited her slavish attention, she thought the opposite, and her willingness drew the line at being scolded. Her looks were not useful enough in the circumstances – he had equally good-looking girls queueing up for his favours. After a year of it she instructed her solicitors to arrange a divorce.

Barbara reverted to her maiden name. She was Barbara Yockenthwaite again, and proud of it since every letter spelt money. She did not count her shekels, had modest tastes, and still had a lot to learn about spending; but her millions had shouldered their way into her psyche, and she could no longer forget who she was. A metaphor describes the self she was growing into: however deep the water she might be in, and however wild the waves that were capable of drowning other people, her toes could always touch base, the solid worth of her gold.

She tried to, she intended to, live at Goose Farm, the home of her English forebears, and the source of her treasure. She had Dorothy Wilson in attendance, cook, housekeeper, chauffeur, gardener and odd job man. She trotted about on a pony, swam in the pool; shopped in Teasham, watched TV; but she was eighteen, then nineteen, and she was hard up for love. Her body had been woken and refused to go back to sleep. She was energetic in all respects, and to be a queen amongst her respectful subjects and servants was no fun. Charities detected her and invited her to functions. Men sniffed her out, introduced themselves, pursued, stalked, propositioned and proposed, but they were the wrong sort, and the women were worse. They were all financial leeches. They were the gold diggers of one sort and another, hosts and hostesses wishing her to add glitter to their parties, poor people begging for handouts, rich people aspiring to be richer. They were the matchmakers and auctioneers of society, hoping to profit from disposing of her in one way or another, and they were the hound-dogs that hunted for cash. She had learnt to recognise and see through them;

but she was lonely, and she chose to be cooperative and generous. She scattered largesse, even after it proved to be never enough.

She ran away to Germany, and news of her cheque book went ahead of her. She spent money, she bought things from men, pictures, works of art; but she was really buying the men, usually in vain. She bought protection rather than love. And she was almost sick of sex, her money always seemed to come between her and her lovers. She suspected they were actually grinding axes instead of concentrating on the job in hand, and they accused her of being absent-minded verging on frigid.

One day Mr Chimbley rang her doorbell. He said he had written letters and made telephone calls, but had received no responses, so had travelled over to Germany to investigate. She invited him to stay, but he said no, he and his wife would be proceeding to spend a few days in Switzerland, at Klosters – yes, for the skiing – and he requested no more than ten minutes of her time in which to talk business. She made a moue with her lips, indicative of a pretty show of reluctance and boredom, and tried to listen and attend.

Mr Chimbley was sorry to inform her that she was spending more than she could afford. She was spending capital as well as income. He backed up his gloomy warnings by references to death duty, income tax, capital gains tax, tax on gifts, and the possibility of a wealth tax. At least financial embarrassment was on her cards, he said. He urged her to economise and retrench before there was a crash.

Barbara was scared. Her solicitor's incomprehensible words were like ghosts, the ghosts of poverty, and they haunted her. She got rid of Mr Chimbley, but could not rid herself of his terrifying hints and insinuations. Perhaps her life had been a vacuum, and he had come and filled it with money. She could not bear to cease to be a multimillionairess. She was addicted to being rich. She realised that she loved what she had begun by not caring for. Poverty was at once unthinkable and all too real in her imagination. She could imagine the agony of not being able to buy whatever she wanted. What would she do without her wealth? She would be 'unemployed': she would have nothing to do. She had regarded her matutinal telephone calls, elaborate beauty treatments, prolonged lunches, afternoon shopping, cocktails and dinner parties and maybe dancing thrown in, as her job. She saw the alternative, working for her living or not working for it, as damnation and death.

Fear propelled her into the arms of Lloyd Jenkinson. He was the treasurer of one of the charities she supported. He was a heavily built man with a red face and reddish hair, in his late thirties, unmarried, and under the impression that he was a Don Juan. He would approach women with an oral click such as horsemen employ to encourage their steeds to go faster: in his case the clicks were meant to be a compliment, and might have encouraged some women not to be slow to respond to his overtures. He was good at mixing dry martinis in a cocktail shaker; a slinky dancer who knew where his leg should go; a raconteur never short of a story to tell; and supposedly a social asset – according to a current witticism no doubt devised by envy and spite, an asset with a heavy accent on the first syllable.

Lloyd had clicked at Barbara. She was unmoved – she thought he was suffering from an impediment. But she danced with him at charity balls, she let him dance with her as he pleased, suffocatingly close with his right hand too low on her back. Then Mr Chimbley paid his visit, and shortly afterwards, at a five course feast which was somehow raising money for handicapped orphans, she sat next to and confided in Lloyd. She said she was miserable. She told him how rich she was or had been. To her surprise he said he knew it.

He not only knew roughly, he knew in detail, the Shadrach connection and her father's business.

She said: 'You know a lot.'

'Knowing's worth money,' he replied.

'Do you know how worried I am?'

'That's a laugh.'

'What do you mean?'

'I could double your income and your capital if you'd let me.'

'No – impossible – I don't believe you.'

'Quite a few people have had to apologise for saying I couldn't solve their financial problems.'

'Could you do the impossible for me?'

'On conditions.'

'Tell me more!'

'Love would oil the wheel of the money mill.'

'Oh love!'

'I've had my eye on you, Barbara. And you should look at me again, because your money combined with mine would enable us to move mountains.'

'Do I want to move mountains?'

'Why not? We could make shares go up and down because of the size of our investments. That's how to make money without tears.'

'Is it legal?'

'Wealth is subject to laws of its own.'

'Is that true?'

'I could prove it to you, so long as you don't forget my conditions.'

She laughed and shrugged her shoulders.

But she met him again accidentally and found him more interesting. She agreed to dine out with him. She invited him to dinner. And they dined alone and one thing led to another.

She had been reassured by the fact that he was nothing like Gerard Bollini. He was certainly the opposite sexually: he was a slow starter and late to cross the finishing line. At least he took gentlemanly precautions, and she never 'lost her head' – after all, it was more business than pleasure. She had agreed beforehand to be his wife. Afterwards, soon, it was too late to say no, and they were duly married in church.

The thrills of being Lloyd's wife were inspired by pieces of paper rather than by physical communion. He brought home in the evening print-outs of their combined portfolios. She could see for herself that the lines of numerals on the last pages of the valuations were getting longer. He would entertain her by telling her what she could afford to buy, a stately home, a grapefruit farm, a private jet, a diamond of multiple carats. She joined him in gloating. She could not have been wrong to be secure for life.

The trouble was that the costs of Lloyd seemed to be beyond her means. He displeased her constantly. He was absent at work for too long, and spent hours on the telephone at home – he was the slave of money instead of herself. He was a fusspot, he worried her about interior decoration, her clothes, her hair, her occasional lapse into a Germanic pronunciation of English words, also his health, his snobbishness, his cars. He was a martinet – the playboy image was reserved for social occasions. He clicked at other women if they looked as if they were willing to click back, Barbara felt like telling them they would be wasting their time.

She was disillusioned. She was on the point of convincing herself that money is not everything. She had thought it would reinforce her beauty, and guarantee that she was and would be the heroine of romance. It had done her not much good with Gerard Bollini, and less with Lloyd Jenkinson. Other men made her feel that she was and would be the pig in the middle between them and her money. She was fed up with the poor and with the charities that nagged her to make them richer and herself poorer. She wanted not to be responsible for the irresponsible people. She was bored by the numbers her husband gave her in lieu of love.

Lloyd succeeded in digging his own grave. She was again so rich that she could do without him. She was too rich to have to suffer.

At a party she danced with a youth who looked like a gipsy. She flirted as usual, he reacted with prodigious confidence and force. He made love to her under scented bushes in the moonlit garden.

He said: 'Shall we run away together?'

They laughed, they were driven by her chauffeur to the airport, where she bought them day clothes and first class one-way tickets to Rio.

He was Dai Williams. He belonged to a Welsh family. He was a teenager, a child in most ways, a man to an extreme degree in one. He was indefatigable. She nicknamed him Pan. They stayed in the grandest hotel, and had much room service and not much sea and sky. Barbara was pleased with him, if exhausted; but she soon realised he was not to be the love of her life.

She took him to the Casino. He gambled away thousands of pounds of her money. She smelt danger. He annoyed her in three other ways, his interest in roulette began to be exclusive; he fretted about having to tell his family where he was and why; and he reminded her of the existence of Lloyd – 'Shouldn't you get in touch with him?'

One morning after an affectionate breakfast she dressed in some of the outdoor clothes she had bought – no dawdling in and out of her nightie.

He expressed surprise.

She told him: 'The party's over.'

His feelings were hurt. His eyes filled with tears. She cheered him up with a cheque that would give him the price of an economy ticket to Wales.

Her reunion with Lloyd was nothing but trouble. He called her names, and said he would only swap a divorce for a hefty percentage of her capital: most of the money he had made for her. She agreed without demur – her impression was that she had struck the better bargain.

She consoled herself by booking into a cruise to the isles of Greece: she was thinking of Byron. Goose Farm was not an option for her, Dorothy was living there and deeply disturbed by Barbara's marital misadventures.

On the cruise she met Gerald Fellowes, and they formed a friendship. He did not look Byronic, he had soft brown hair and a long neck, but he too was a poet or aiming to head in that direction. His story was a romance such as Barbara had wished to be involved in. His mother, sister and brother had contributed to the costs of his cruise – they shared his belief that exposure to the culture of Ancient Greece would reinforce his literary vocation and unlock his poetic power.

His family was far from rich, and the even more touching aspect of the generosity of three members of it was that they were all afflicted with tuberculosis. His late father had died of the disease.

In the evenings, after Gerald had done the excursion of the day and Barbara had perhaps had a swim or watched a film, they would sit side by side on deck, watching the sun go down and summon stars into the dark blue sky.

He read her his poems in a voice lowered to a soulful whisper. She could not hear everything, and what she could hear was hard to understand; on the other hand his whispering in her ear compensated. She often invited him to dine with her. Once there was dancing and she taught him how to hold her. Still more touching and attractive in her estimation was his marvelling at the comfort of the cruise ship, the luxury of his cabin and the big meals served four times a day, all of which she could have bought for him a thousand times over. She loved him for informing her of the power she wielded potentially. He made her feel like the good fairy in the pantomime.

She loved him for one other reason. She hesitated to give him money that would change his life and probably destroy his fragile inclinations to be a poet. She had experience of the ambiguity of money. Should she spare him the wherewithal to pay his debts, care for his ailing relations, and live the usually unrewarding life of an artist? She was happy to think she was not a wicked woman, she wished to do right by Gerald Fellowes.

One evening towards the end of the cruise they sat out on deck after dinner. It was a balmy night with silver reflections of the moon in the sea. He said how happy he was and had been, and asked if she felt the same.

Instead of answering, she asked a different question: 'How do you think I can afford to be cruising like this?'

He did not know.

'I'm rich.'

He said he was glad.

'You've no idea of how rich I am, Gerald. You and I live on different planets, financially speaking. There are light years between us.'

He was denying it, but she interrupted.

'You don't know what I'm talking about – it doesn't matter – but I don't want to be misunderstood. I'd like to give you enough money to repay your family, buy the best treatment for your ill relations, and have time for your poetry to come into its own. There! It's an offer, and I hope you're not too proud to accept it.'

Disbelief was succeeded by gratitude, by hugs that turned into embraces, kisses that started in one way and ended in another, and in short to protracted cuddles in her state cabin and then marriage on dry land.

It was a romantic fiasco. She spoiled him. He did no work of any sort, he was lazy. His mother and siblings were venal as well as tubercular, also art snobs – on the telephone they patronised Barbara, and revealed that they were socialists. She sailed away on another cruise, it went to the Far East, and delegated the task of obliterating the error of her third husband to Mr Chimbley.

Barbara Yockenthwaite, to which name she had reverted, formed another close friendship on board. It was with a smart American lady of Hungarian extraction, Mrs Longrigg, whose Christian name was unexpectedly – considering her feminine appearance and daintiness – Charley. Charley Longrigg was Barbara's contemporary, a divorcee, and rich too – they quickly established that each of them had more money than they could count. They agreed that it was a great relief not to be making friends with persons who were less well off and more likely to be resentful. They talked easily and freely of their marriages. Charley was disgusted by men, she said; and Barbara was tempted to say, 'Snap!' They dined together and spoke of clothes, hairdressers, make-up and hotels. Shortly before they reached Hong Kong, on a day of foul weather when the decks were flooded with sea spray, they also joined forces for lunch. On the way out of the first-class restaurant Charley took Barbara's hand and caressed the palm in a suggestive way.

In her plaintive little voice she asked: 'What are you thinking of doing this afternoon?'

Barbara withdrew her hand and replied firmly: 'I'm going to my cabin, I'm going to pack my cases.'

Charley persisted.

'Aren't you ever lonely? I get so lonely – can I come with you?'

'No – no – sorry,' Barbara answered and escaped.

She was upset not so much by the sexual innuendo as by the confession of loneliness. She had uttered a denial, but her no had referred to Charley's plea for company, not to the other question. It brought home to her how lonely she was and had almost always been, and that her wealth had formed a barrier to all forms of intercourse. A new horror loomed cloud-like over her imagination. She saw years ahead, her forties, her fifties, age, isolation that would be frightful if she was rich, unbearable if not.

In Hong Kong the cruise ship with Charley aboard continued on its way, and Barbara took refuge in the Mandarin Hotel. She bought clothes and shoes, and ate alone in her suite. Her loneliness was horrible, and she did not know how to alleviate her pain or if she could stand long years of nothingness. She had her hair done daily, and a minor facelift. She confided in a girl who gave her beauty treatments in her hotel room. The girl was Asian, gentle and sympathetic – Barbara never knew her name. She recommended a medicine man, perhaps doctor, versed in the wisdom and the ancient therapies of the East, who was also a prince of somewhere. Barbara obtained a telephone number, made an appointment and reported to a penthouse flat in a multi-storey building not far from her hotel.

The door of the flat was opened by Asian girls in brilliantly coloured national costumes.

They smiled and giggled and escorted Barbara into a large room or open space leading to a balcony full of heavy-leaved plants. Chinese scripts lined the walls, deep carpets and rugs were underfoot, the air was scented, and a man sat behind a vast desk at a distance. She sat on a chair opposite him – no one told her to, she seated herself in silence. He stared at her and frightened her.

Prince Jan-Thai Svendahl was brown-skinned, with long straight black hair, and wore a white medical-type jacket, and a large jewel dangled on to his chest. He might be in his thirties.

At last he spoke. His voice was silky. He immediately asked her personal questions, and she was surprised that she answered them. His English was good but accented. He sat very still and took no notes.

After however long it was he told her: 'I can help you. I can make you stronger. You would feel younger. But my treatment is very expensive.'

'The expense doesn't matter to me.'

'It would matter to me,' he replied, 'if you were unable to pay for my services.'

'I have millions of pounds.'

'You would have to spend time, too, time at my sanatorium, The Wishing Well.'

'I see.'

'How much do you want to find love and happiness again?'

'Very much – I've never found happiness – I'd give anything for that.'

'It can be yours. Thank you for seeking me.

Speak to my assistants – they will arrange everything.'

He stood up. There was no question of a handshake. The door was opened for her to leave his presence. A stern middle-aged Chinese woman in an anteroom spoke to her of dates, travel to The Wishing Well in Thailand, and asked for money for tickets and an advance of fees for treatment – Barbara wrote a cheque for ten thousand pounds.

Out in the street she shook her head as if to efface the memory of a dream – or was it a nightmare? She wondered if she had been hypnotised. Was she playing with fire? She felt she had signed on to join the historic regiment of ageing women who volunteer to be fleeced by rogues. Yet she had been offered excitement, and that was what she pined for now, novelty, even danger – she had sampled every other pleasure.

She arrived at The Wishing Well. She was shown into a luxury chalet. It had a small walled garden with a blue swimming pool. The white-coated Asian man who showed her into it explained that Professor Prince Jan-Thai would treat her in the afternoon of the next day. Meanwhile, it was part of her treatment that she should stay in her chalet until two o'clock on the following afternoon, receive vegetarian meals, listen to music, experience solitude, and rest.

Barbara was bored stiff by a couple of hours

of resting. She hated the silence and could not fancy the food. Time dragged by, and she decided to call it a day. There was no telephone and her door was locked. The girls who brought her meals did not understand her requests, her anger, and blocked her exit, giggling. Her suspicions gravitated into fright. But she felt it would be undignified to scream and yell, and that she had to see her adventure through.

The man in white appeared eventually. He was polite and charming, sympathised with the difficulties she complained of, and said they were 'normal'. She was led along paths and passages, and other assistants were all smiles and ushered her into a large scented space. It could be a conservatory, but one end looked like an operating theatre. Her doctor or guru or whatever he was greeted her with solemn courtesy and softly-spoken commands, which in spite of herself she obeyed.

'Come over here, please – lie on the massage table – roll up your sleeve! I am going to give you an injection of vitamins and a trace of relaxant. Call me Prince. I will call you Barbara. You must not be embarrassed by my treatment, which is based upon freedom from inhibitions. Take off your blouse, I shall begin with massage.'

It was the beginning of the end of Barbara Yockenthwaite. She was drugged, but not enough: she knew her clothes were removed and his massage stopped nowhere. She was subjected to acupuncture productive of involuntary sexual responses, and further mechanical stimulation. His more personal usage of her body was perverse.

She never recovered her wits. Drugs and sex kept her in a state of mindless passivity. Her Prince praised her beauty as she lost weight and weakened. She signed the cheques and the papers that were laid before her. She laughed at what she was doing and was being done to her. At some stage she went through a ceremony of sorts, and was later told she had become Princess Jan-Thai Svendahl. She tried to speak about her father who had called her Baaarbra, and Germany and Goose Farm, and she cried a lot, but nobody heard her, nobody bothered, and she was settled down by means of another injection.

At some stage, after uncounted weeks or months, she was disturbed by loud voices and an altercation. She was in her swimming pool, and an English woman and a man entered her chalet in spite of the white-coated assistants' efforts to restrain them. They advanced on to her patio and spoke as she stood in the blue water, naked and only vaguely registering their presence.

'Barbara, Barbara,' the woman cried out, and the man called, 'Miss Yockenthwaite!'

They were Dorothy Wilson and Morgan Chimbley.

Barbara said: 'I'm Princess Jan-Thai.'

'Oh Barbara, Barbara dear, come home – we have a court order!'

Mr Chimbley explained: 'We have the right to ask you if you would like to come home to England.'

'No,' she said.

'Oh Barbara, do you remember me, I'm Dorothy – all your money's gone, they've stolen it – but if you come home I'll look after you, I will.'

'No,' she said.

'Miss Yockenthwaite ...' Mr Chimbley began.

'Who's she?' Barbara interrupted. 'I wish you'd go away. I'm finished. Goodbye!'

'No, Barbara, please,' Dorothy begged, 'please – you look so ill – I'll make you better.'

Barbara spoke to the assistants who were lurking in the background.

'Take these people out of my sight.'

Dorothy protested and Mr Chimbley waved a piece of paper at Barbara.

She submerged herself in the water.

On the other side of the world some days later, Morgan Chimbley received from the British Consulate in Thailand notification of the death of Barbara, formerly Kuchenmacher, Yockenthwaite, Bollini, Jenkinson and finally Jan-Thai Svendahl, Princess.

Consequently he had something to say to Heather when they had retired to bed.

'That Yockenthwaite woman died. She was penniless in the end.'

'How tragic! Penniless!' Heather commented. 'Have you been paid for your trouble, dear?'

'I'm a professional man, Heather. That's my answer to your question. A sum is set aside in the Chimbley-Yockenthwaite account to cover emergencies. I have been thinking of Dorothy Wilson, who was appointed by the "cakemaker" to keep an eye on his daughter. She accompanied me to Thailand, and she explained that she had not been paid by Barbara for a long time.'

'Morgan, I do hope you have not been thinking of her in the wrong way.'

'Certainly not. My thoughts were charitable. Perhaps Dorothy should receive a gratuity from the Chimbley-Yockenthwaite fund.'

'How much, are you thinking?'

'Ten thousand pounds, maybe.'

'Surely five or even two would be sufficient? Hasn't she been living scot-free at Goose Farm for all this time?'

'True!'

'You never know when money will be needed for the next emergency.'

'Thank you for your foresight, Heather. You have a brain after my own heart.'

Seventh Chapter of Nine

Morgan Chimbley entertained an uncharacteristic wish. It was momentary and shocking. He wished that his path and Shadrach Yockenthwaite's had never crossed. He was sated by the biographies of Shadrach's heirs, who had all come to grief and more or less early graves. Coincidence had run amok in the Yockenthwaite clan. Curses and black arts were not so much to blame as stupidity. Morgan was moved by the wastefulness. He felt nauseous to remember the money that had been poured down the drain, millions of it, multimillions. He was not sure he could bear to give away more money that would be frittered and scattered. He mourned the money he had been instrumental in losing. He wondered if he would have the strength of mind to refer a new bequest and its management to a colleague in the family firm. He half-hoped never again to hear that word, Yockenthwaite.

His hope was dashed. Luckily he recovered his common sense and professionalism in the nick of time. Ten million, give or take a million, arrived in the offices of Chimbley Chimbley and Davis. They came from the Isle of Man. The uncertainty as to the exact sum was largely due to solicitors' fees.

Mr Chimbley inserted advertisements in the customary papers. He did so again, then again. At last a letter from a Clifford Macdonald in Hobart, Tasmania, reached him. Mr Macdonald tried to explain his relationship with Shadrach in prose so complex as to be incomprehensible, and asked what Mr Chimbley had meant by 'advantage'. Mr Macdonald's question was more of a demand: 'What would be to my advantage, tell me that!'

Mr Chimbley's antennae twitched. He was not used to being ordered about, and his suspicions were aroused by the incivility. He did not explain himself in his letter to Mr Macdonald, he just set out the need of a DNA test proving kinship.

Mr Macdonald's answer was again unsatisfactory. He wrote that he would not travel to England on a wild goose chase, he was too busy, and he doubted that Mr Chimbley's 'advantage' would be advantageous to a high earner like himself. Moreover he thought the DNA test was cheeky. All the same, as he was accustomed to not leaving stones unturned, he was ready to send a sample of his blood to the solicitor. He would send it in a freezer bag by air, and the authenticity of the blood would be attested to by Dr Horace Wang, English-trained and working in the best Tasmanian hospital, and Ronald Wapshott, a lawyer, a Hobart councillor, a highly respected Tasmanian citizen and a perfect gentleman. Was it a deal?

Mr Chimbley sought advice from his colleagues. He was wary of Mr Macdonald's boastfulness and bad manners; but he could be wrong, and

158

the alternative to giving him the benefit of the doubt was that Chimbley Chimbley and Davis would be stuck with millions of unusable pounds. He explained further. He could not advertise again – Mr Macdonald would apply. Should he insist on Mr Macdonald flying round the world to take a blood test under proper supervision? Should he in person travel to Tasmania with a doctor in tow? Above all, the question that mattered most: was it the last tranche of Shadrach's money? If it was, and Mr Macdonald were bypassed, the solicitors could keep it and divide it amongst themselves. If it was not, and still more money was on the way, who would deserve to get that? Old Mr Chimbley was bewildered, slightly younger Mr Davis shook his head, and Morgan Chimbley had to decide.

He wrote in the affirmative. Yes, it was a deal, and he therefore awaited the arrival of the blood sample with interest. The test was passed, and in due course Clifford Macdonald was ushered into the solicitor's office without further delay.

He was middle-aged – Mr Chimbley had expected a younger man. He wore a suit. He was slightly dark-skinned, not just sunburnt, and had a forceful jaw and eyes that seemed to 'narrow'. He had neat greying hair. He appeared to be restless, and averse to wasting time.

'What's the story?' he asked as he sat in the chair on the clients' side of Mr Chimbley's desk.

'We are convinced that you are the rightful heir to some of the estate of Mr Shadrach Yockenthwaite.'

159

'How much?'

'That is hard to say.'

'And that's lawyer language. Talk turkey, if you please.'

'You will be the sixth heir to the estate.'

'Why have I missed out?'

'You did not reply to my advertisement. Your "turkey", sir, will be in the region of ten million pounds.'

'Not bad, ten mill – pays my airline ticket – not bad at all. How much did the other geezers get?'

'Fifty-two million.'

'You're joking.'

'No, sir, I'm not given to jokes when talking about money.'

'I believe you there.'

'You will also inherit Mr Shadrach's home and property, Goose Farm, located not far from here.'

'What's that worth?'

'We don't value property. You would have to ask an estate agent.'

'Guess!'

'Not less than five hundred thousand.'

'Nice, no question! Goose Farm, funny name! How come you got the job of looking after so much money? It's a bit fishy, I'd say, Morgan.'

'Mr Macdonald, I do not accept that sort of talk, but I can understand that you may be startled by your good fortune. If you're prepared to be polite, I'll explain the whys and wherefores of how you have just become richer than you were ten minutes ago.'

'No offence meant – fire ahead!'

'I didn't know your benefactor – he was not known to my firm He died suddenly, in a fire at Goose Farm, the cause of which was never established. He had won a sweepstake of some sort, his winnings amounted to tens of millions of pounds, and, because he was a secretive man by all accounts and extremely careful with his money, he placed it in dated cash accounts in a variety of tax havens. When the first account matured – posthumously, some time after his death – the money arrived here. He must have named our firm to be the recipient of that sum and successive further sums. We – I, to be precise – have passed on each one as it arrived to Mr Shadrach's proven blood relations who had responded to my advertisements in the newspapers. "Fishy", you said – the only "fishy" thing about this sequence of events is that a single claimant answered each of my six advertisements, one applicant only, but I personally ascribe that to coincidence.'

'Okay, but why haven't the others, or at least one of them, applied for the dosh that's almost in my pocket?'

Mr Chimbley cleared his throat.

'There have been accidents,' he said.

'Accidents?'

'Mortal accidents in some cases, also deaths from more or less natural causes.'

'Five of them?'

'I'm sorry to say, at least.'

'Was it the money that did for them?'

161

'I suspect that in roundabout ways it could have contributed to the loss of life.'

'Fishy wasn't far wrong.'

'Luck, good and bad, strikes me as a fairer description.'

'Where's my money? I don't go in for morbidity.'

'Your money's in our local bank, and the manager, Mr Burns, is waiting to receive you today, as soon as we finish here.'

'I won't be dealing with local branches in future.'

'That's your prerogative. Mr Burns will follow your instructions. May I ask if you will want to change your name to Yockenthwaite?'

'Good God, no! What a peculiar notion!'

'Other beneficiaries have done so.'

'I'm not intending to tread in the footsteps of the other beneficiaries, I won't be heading for the cemetery.'

'The present caretaker of Goose Farm is Higgins – he took over from Miss Dorothy Wilson, who retired. He occupies a flat converted from a stable on the property. He also is ready to receive you at your convenience. I have his telephone number and mobile number, they're amongst the papers I shall be handing over to you, together with keys. Some signatures will be required. Would you like me to ring Mr Higgins to make an appointment for you to see Goose Farm?'

'I'm not alone, sir.'

'Sorry?'

'I have a partner. And I'm just thinking.'

'Are you in partnership with another business-man?'

'You're barking up the wrong tree, Morgan.'

'I'm sorry, sir.'

'Call me Cliff, for pity's sake.'

'As you wish.'

'My partner's the female variety. She's with me.'

'In England, do you mean? Or in this building?'

'She could be out in your waiting room by now. She was having a mosey round the town.'

'Shall I ask her to join us?'

'You'll do no such thing. Tell me, we're not wired here, are we?'

'Beg pardon?'

'You're not recording our conversation?'

'Certainly not! Our services are strictly confidential.'

'Is that a solemn promise?'

'It's a fact, and my fact is the equal of a promise.'

'Very well. My partner's called Mrs Stephenson, Mrs Joy Stephenson. I respect her and expect her to be respected, but that's not to say she's entitled to know my financial business. My finances are private. You get my drift?'

'I do.'

'The money you hold for me will soon be mine, you will not know what I do with it, and you and your colleagues will have to forget that it was ever in your keeping.'

'Understood, sir.'

'My name's Cliff.'

'Yes, Cliff.'

'The same applies to the bank manager.'

'Mr Burns is an eminently discreet man, and his staff is of high quality.'

'They'd better be. Now, you referred to a sum of money "in the region" of ten million. Let's have some precision.'

'Well, first of all, I have not had a chance to mention tax. Your inheritance could be liable for tax at forty per cent.'

'Other people have tried to rob me.'

'Our Inland Revenue is not noted for its obliging character.'

'That makes two of us. We'll see who turns tail when we go head to head. Any other loose ends?'

'My firm has been paying Mr Higgins for caretaking at Goose Farm, and has also paid bills for maintenance. We have held money in a separate account to deal with such outgoings. Would you wish us to continue to do so and to keep an adequate sum that we can draw on as required?'

'Yes and no – continue until I tell you to stop – and then I'll require itemised accounts.'

Mr Chimbley coughed.

'I see,' he said.

'Anything else?'

'Our fee, yes. We have deducted it from the principal as time has passed, and there will be a final reckoning when the handover is complete.'

'I don't like the sound of that.'

'We charge in accordance with the rights of our profession.'

'I'm not a soft touch, Morgan.'

'You have made it very clear to me, Cliff. Shall I escort you along to the bank?'

'What would it cost me? No, sirree!'

Mr Chimbley was not above being mildly interested in human stories, he would entertain Heather with his descriptions of clients or a peculiar will; but all sorts and conditions of men, and women for that matter, were reduced to fees by sitting in the chair on the far side of his desk. He was impervious to beauty, charm or physical imperfections. That was his rule, but Clifford Macdonald was the inevitable exception. Cliff had inspired only negative responses. He was unpleasant and ungrateful. He had taken his millions almost for granted, as if he got his hands on such sums on a daily basis. He was altogether too calm in an excitable situation. He was either so rich that the extra money did not matter, or poor and putting on an act. He was surely not to be trusted. What was he, what were the defining characteristics of Tasmanians? Was the creature called the Tasmanian Devil a clue of some description?

Mr Chimbley was ashamed of his almost superstitious reaction to the man who had left his premises wheeling a suitcase like any other traveller. But before his working day was done he received a telephone call from Mr Burns.

'The plot has thickened today' – this was the bank manager's greeting.

'Do you speak,' Mr Chimbley queried in reply, 'of Clifford Macdonald?'

'Talk about strangers! He's a stranger and no mistake. Is he a genuine Yockenthwaite?'

'He seems to have the same DNA.'

'Seems? I thought that test was infallible.'

'He had it done in Tasmania. We accepted its authenticity under pressure.'

'Is he a fraud? I wouldn't be surprised if he was.'

'God knows!'

'The other strange thing, if he should happen to be an impostor or crook, is that he's more like Shadrach Yockenthwaite than any of the other beneficiaries. He's just about as disagreeable.'

'How did he behave in the bank?'

'He was arrogant. He treated us like his serfs. He went through our charges with a toothcomb and bullied us into cancelling some. He wanted preparations made for the transfer of nearly all his assets to a bank elsewhere. He didn't hit anyone, but he upset us all. And I'm in the wrong to be leaking this information.'

'Your experience matches mine. His first question to me was, "What's the story?" You and I will now be looking out for the next chapter. Isn't that so?'

'Exactly.'

It was spoken, the next chapter, by Higgins from Goose Farm. He rang Mr Chimbley to say that the gentleman and his lady, Cliff and Joy, as he had been ordered to call them, had arrived late, stayed for two nights, and now left in their new car.

'Did you say the car's new?'

166

'I did, sir – Mercedes saloon, gold colour and brand new.'

'He hasn't wasted much time, has he? Money yesterday, luxury car today. What's Mrs Stephenson like?'

'She's Australian, she was wearing white gloves.'

'What's the rest of her like?'

'Oh, pretty, lots of hair, blonde, and a sharp eye, too.'

'Was he okay with you?'

'He said he had big plans for Goose Farm, but I could carry on as odd-job man.'

'What about your pay?'

'He said I'd receive it from the bank.'

'Did you believe him?'

'I'll have to wait and see – I've nowhere else to go.'

'Let's hope he's trustworthy.'

'Yes, sir. I was forgetting to say – he had a man out here to value the property.'

Mr Chimbley was soon on the receiving end of another surprise. He received an address or change of address notice. Embossed on the gilt-edged card was the legend: Clifford Macdonald, Finance and Property – and his Head Office was a penthouse in the West End of London, with half a dozen telephone numbers and other means of communication listed, fax, email, voice-mail and website.

Then, at a meeting of the Rotary Club of Teasham, Mr Chimbley came across the man who had valued Goose Farm, Bob Welling from Welling and Sturdy, estate agents.

Morgan and Bob were old acquaintances, Morgan had pushed remunerative opportunities Bob's way, and Bob was aware of the outline of the Shadrach Yockenthwaite inheritance.

'I had a call from a customer of yours the other day,' Bob said.

'Oh yes?' Morgan queried.

'Mr Macdonald, Cliff, as I was asked to call him. He wanted to know the value of Goose Farm, the Yockenthwaite place.'

'What did you tell him?'

'Three parts of a brick.'

'As much as that?'

'Could be more – money's been spent on it in recent years, enough to make old Shadrach turn in his grave.'

They laughed.

'What's Cliff up to? Is he looking for a sale?' Morgan asked.

'No – nothing like – could be a loan.'

'Ah!'

'Might be wanting to borrow money against collateral of property.'

'But I'd handed him millions on a plate an hour or two before you say he was holding out the begging bowl.'

'He's a dark one, all for the money, no doubt about it. He asked me to look for a tenant of Goose Farm ready to pay top rent.'

'Did he offer any sort of explanation?'

'He said something funny. He said, "I could be milking two cows here" – something like that.'

168

'Borrowing against Goose Farm, and receiving rent from letting Goose Farm, he must have meant.'

'Could well be.'

Some days later Mr Chimbley met Mr Burns in the multi-storey carpark.

They exchanged greetings, and Mr Burns inquired: 'Have you had any more truck with Clifford Macdonald?'

'Not exactly. Have you?'

'I've signed an affidavit from a loan company, he's trying to borrow two hundred thousand pounds.'

'I heard a rumour. The sum's much larger than I expected. What did you sign?'

'I ticked the answer to a question. They were asking me if he could afford to pay the interest on his loan for twelve months.'

'What was the interest?'

'Interest rates are low at the moment, he could have got a loan cheap.'

'He's letting Goose Farm.'

'Good gracious! Why, for heaven's sake?'

'The rent would pay the interest on the loan.'

'But he's rolling in money,' Mr Burns remarked disapprovingly.

'Did you receive his change of address card?'

'Oh yes – yes – I suppose that explains it – gambling in property.'

'And we'll be picking up the pieces.'

'Probably,' Mr Burns agreed.

The estate agent Bob Welling had more to say to Mr Chimbley on the subject of Cliff

Macdonald. At another Rotary meeting he passed on the information that Goose Farm had been let to Arab people for a monthly fortune, and secondly that Cliff had bought an entire terrace of newbuild houses, twelve of them, still awaiting kitchen installations, for a large sum of money. Apparently he was intending to rent them out.

Time passed.

One morning Mr Chimbley ushered a female client into his room and on to the chair by his desk. She was Joy Stephenson, who had made an appointment. She was still showing signs of wanting to attract attention, with her gilded hair, clever make-up, and bold upright posture. She was well-dressed in coat and skirt, not in slovenly English fashion. She smiled sweetly and betrayed the inclination to laugh which is women's secret weapon.

Mr Chimbley had not known whether or not to grant her an audience. He felt that to do so might be unethical, because she was only the partner of his client; on the other hand Cliff had insisted that she was to be respected.

'What can I do for you?' he inquired.

She bridled slightly. She would love to have a little advice, she said. She hoped not to take up too much of his precious time.

Mr Chimbley decided not to reveal quite how precious his time was, hoping that Cliff might pay up even if she did not.

'My "partner",' – she pronounced the word as if it was so inadequate as to deserve the ridicule of inverted commas – 'inherited money, I believe.'

Mr Chimbley maintained a stubborn silence.

'He seems to have struck lucky. He has a spring in his step these days. To tell the truth, he's spending money like a drunken sailor. He's in a hyperactive phase, that's a fact.'

Mr Chimbley cleared his throat.

'I cannot be to blame for his state of health, Mrs Stephenson,' he said.

'Oh Mr Chimbley, I'm not here to angle for an apology. You might have misunderstood me. I would love to have help, if you'd be so kind. Shall I come to the point?'

He nodded in an encouraging manner.

'I've given Cliff a good slice of my life. It hasn't always been in Easy Street. We've shared alike. Now, it's what's his is no-one else's. He's a changed man, but I can change, too. Do I look like a doormat, Mr Chimbley? I've always had other options. Cliff's said to me "Later, later" once too often. I'd like my share right away. I'm not going to be a pauper willingly. Are you with me?'

'I am, Mrs Stephenson, which is not to say I could help you.'

'Has he made a will?'

'No.'

'You could suggest a will.'

'I could bear it in mind.'

'Thank you, Mr Chimbley. Of course you can't do more, and it wouldn't be right for me to ask you to plead my cause. I'm really here to protect Cliff, not myself. And you could help both of us. Leading questions are out, I'm aware

171

of that, but my mental arithmetic tells me that Cliff must have spent millions, many millions on property and stuff, and my question to you is this, will he be in trouble or bankrupt?'

Mr Chimbley replied: 'I can set your mind at rest, Mrs Stephenson, and I cannot say more than that.'

He was thanked, was asked to call her Joy, kissed goodbye, and left to wonder how far he had been twisted round her little finger.

Shortly afterwards an item of junk mail arrived at Chimbley Chimbley and Davis. It advertised Cliff Macdonald's Charitable Trust of Affordable Housing for Hard-working Families, donations welcome. A stamped addressed envelope was enclosed.

Morgan Chimbley was in his office. He was taking time off to read his legal newspaper – he could afford to do so. He reacted to one notice with a wintry smile. The notice related that the Inland Revenue was summoning Mr Clifford Macdonald, the Antipodean multimillionaire and philanthropist, for non-payment of tax: he was apparently owing twenty million pounds. The exaggeration amused the solicitor: he was a collector of journalistic errors. A longer article, including an interview with Mr Macdonald, also amused the solicitor. Cliff had told the reporter that he was almost the opposite of a multi-millionaire, that nearly all his money had been spent on housing the homeless and trying to repair the damage done to the poor and handi-capped by the UK's merciless social system. He quoted the numbers of those who had benefited from his charitable organisation. He drew attention to the families that had previously been stuffed into one-room flats or the crypts of churches, whom he had moved into clean modern cheap rented houses in the constituencies of the Prime Minister and his ministers. He declared that the Inland Revenue was attempting by means of irrelevant laws to have our weakest and most pitiable fellow-citizens thrown out of their homes and on to the streets of this wealthy country.

A publicity campaign followed. Cliff bought advertising space, and trumpeted the message that he was the knight in shining armour riding to the rescue of casualties of rampant capitalism, he was Robin Hood, and he needed the wherewithal to do battle with the oppressor. Donation forms must have been filled in. Fancy figures of money contributed were published on a weekly basis. Cliff knew his onions. He knew that everybody except the politicians hated the tax-gatherers, they always had. He also understood that public opinion likes to hear about a moneyed man losing money: he plugged the news that he had had to move his Charitable Trust out of the penthouse in West One and into temporary accommodation in the East End.

The Inland Revenue served its Final Demand, and Cliff launched his appeal. He began to appear on TV, sometimes alone with black bags under his eyes, sometimes with an attractive little family of parents and well-behaved children that was near the top of the list of probable expulsions from enviable Macdonald dwellings. Celebrities stood up to be counted alongside the Tasmanian hero. There was a demo outside the Houses of Parliament.

Cliff played his game cleverly, the Inland Revenue showed itself to be hard-hearted, disagreeable and stupid. A fire-eating journalist was called up by the powers-that-be to tear the offender limb from limb on a news programme. Cliff dodged him successfully. He explained that he had applied to become a Registered Charity, but his application would not be ratified until the Inland Revenue desisted from harassing him. In reply to questions about the penthouse, which was not exactly a suitable address for somebody posing as a male version of Mother Theresa, he explained that he had been the guest of Mrs Stephenson, an Australian friend from way back and a supporter of his work for the unfortunates, who was either the owner or the tenant of the apartment.

The legal battle ran true to form, it dragged on. But time also brought it to an end, or rather the beginning of the end. Both sides doubtless counted their mounting costs, the Inland Revenue thought they were getting the worst of it, and Cliff was afraid he might have had the best. A compromise was arrived at in some lordly court: Cliff would pay part of the tax due, but not all his liabilities.

Mr Chimbley read about Clifford Macdonald's

victory, and suspected it was more like defeat. The economic news was that inflation threatened, interest rates would rise, and the borrowers of money would be in trouble. Householders could find their mortgages unaffordable, and property tycoons wonder where the next big meal was coming from. Mr Chimbley was not alone in guessing the effects on the Charitable Trust. He read a report that Mrs Joy Stephenson was suing Cliff for a swingeing amount of palimony, millions of pounds: she must have decided to strike while the iron was still warm.

What was not expected was Cliff's return to Chimbley Chimbley and Davis. He arrived at midday, and marched into the office of Mr Morgan Chimbley, who made as much of a virtue as possible of the precaution of seating intruders in the chair reserved for clients.

He felt he had to: but Cliff was not the forceful man he had been. He was redder in the face and wheezed. He looked ill. He looked disreputable, like a seedy bookmaker, and shifty, as if he was waiting for the hand of the law on his shoulder. His suit was familiar, it might have been the one he wore during his previous visit, but it was crumpled, even stained; and the top button of his shirt was undone and his tie resembled a loose halter. At the same time he seemed more human and accessible than he had been.

'Well, Morgan,' he remarked, 'How's tricks? Do you read the scandal-sheets?'

Mr Chimbley mumbled sympathetically.

'I didn't deserve my good luck, and maybe it's ditto with bad luck. How much money did you give me in this room, ten mill, eleven? I made as much again, even twice as much. Do you know high finance?'

Mr Chimbley made an ambiguous gesture with his head: he was not going to say he knew it inside out.

'Should be called low finance – it's a doddle if you know how. I inherited Goose Farm, and could borrow money against the value of one house and buy two more. I bought hundreds for next to nothing. And people gave me money to turn into more money for them. I made a mountain of money. I had enough mortgages to sink a battleship. They sunk me instead.'

Mr Chimbley looked pained.

'Interest rates went up,' Cliff said, 'and I was dead in the water, financially speaking. Mortgages were too expensive – my houses were repossessed – millions well and truly lost. Heard of my Charitable Trust? I made another mint out of that, and foxed the taxman – I still haven't paid his bill in full. He's after me, they're all after me, I'm a fugitive – and there's another tax on sex.'

Mr Chimbley framed a question that included the name of Mrs Stephenson.

Cliff replied: 'Joy's not a bad old girl. She's no pushover, but she made a mistake when she mixed up with me, and she's making another to touch me for three million – she's missed the boat. That brings me to why I'm here, Morgan. Do me a favour, will you? I want you to be my legal representative, you'll be in sole charge. I aim to go bankrupt.'

Mr Chimbley coughed.

Cliff continued: 'You'll know why. I've got a parcel of debts – see this plastic bag? It's full of bills and threats – I've more debts than I could ever repay. Don't look down your nose, Morgan! I feel sorry for the people I won't pay, I do – but after all I'm not in the wrong according to the laws of the land. You haven't half got some dozy politicians in this country, Morgan! Get a load of debt? – Don't worry, dear! – Go bankrupt, and hey presto, you're not in debt any more – it's weird and wonderful! Well, there it is, a loophole in the law, and I'm climbing through it. You tell them the tale, you establish my bankruptcy, and I'll be grateful – no money available, no trouble, see, and nobody's going to chase me round the world for no gain.'

Mr Chimbley cleared his throat again, and asked: 'How grateful would you be, or could you be?'

'I'm not a pauper, bankruptcy notwithstanding. I've got my nest egg out of reach of authorities – I could put some aside for you. I could even pay in advance.'

'How much would the advance be?'

'A hundred thou.'

'I'm aware that it's possible to get out of trouble by opting for bankruptcy on a temporary or permanent basis. But I might be involved in costly work to do as you ask. I think one hundred and fifty thousand would be more appropriate.'

'I can't do more than a hundred thousand in cash, and I'm not in a position to write a cheque for such a large sum, that's obvious, and you might have problems in accepting such a cheque.'

'Do you have the cash with you?'

'I certainly do.'

'Very well...'

They shook hands across the desk and Morgan inquired: 'I expect you'll be going abroad?'

Cliff winked and produced an airline ticket.

'No harm in jumping the gun,' he said.

They were together for another hour, counting money, going through papers, settling points and exchanging information.

At length Cliff said he had a plane to catch, and they stood up.

Morgan said to Cliff in a friendly way: 'Might I ask you a personal question?'

'Fire ahead.'

'Are you really related to the Yockenthwaites?'

'Not half, as you limeys say.'

'Honestly?'

'The DNA proved it, isn't that right?'

'Not the answer to my question. The Yockenthwaites have a miserly streak. I don't see a miser in you. Were you playing fair?'

'Play's seldom fair. All's fair in love and competition. You didn't check up on Dr Horace Wang and a lawyer called Wapshott. They're imaginative names, don't you think? Anyway, you were satisfied.'

'I wish I hadn't asked you.'

'Water under the bridge, Morgan. Have a nice life! Thanks for the millions. Bye!'

Morgan Chimbley was glad to say goodbye. He hoped it was adieu, and the bad penny would never turn up again. He resented having been made a fool of, it hurt his feelings. Now he was embarrassed by his hundred thousand pounds, although they did ease his sufferings. He stuffed them away in the personal safe in his office, and spent the evening of the day in the bosom of his family.

In the bedroom he told Heather some of the story of Clifford Macdonald.

She said: 'He sounds like an awful crook, dear.'

He told her: 'Cliff has asked me to institute proceedings for bankruptcy. He believes that if he's officially bankrupt he won't be bothered by the tax gatherers or his ex-girlfriend; but I'm not sure a missing person can be bankrupt, and I'm afraid of being embroiled in his dirty tricks.'

'Second thoughts are often the best policy, dear.'

'Thank you, Heather. I shall bear your advice in mind.'

'What's happened to Goose Farm?'

'He sold off bits of it.'

'How terrible!'

'It wouldn't have mattered if he had been the last beneficiary of Shadrach's estate. As things stand I shall have to buy back the bits he sold.'

'Not you yourself, Morgan? It's really nothing to do with you personally.'

'I was deceived, I could be charged with dereliction of duty, and forced to repay the money I allowed Cliff to steal.'

'The firm would have to contribute.'

'Oh no, no, I don't want my colleagues poking their noses into my affairs.'

'Well, Morgan, remember, Shadrach's millions are not yet completely accounted for. There must be more money on the way for you to deal with as you alone see fit. Nobody needs to be any the wiser.'

'Do I catch your meaning, Heather?'

'Shadrach won't notice if he pays for Goose Farm.'

'Well done, Heather - another nail hit on the head!'

Eighth Chapter of Nine

Mr Morgan Chimbley was scarred by Clifford Macdonald. In his private and somewhat illegal opinion, the only virtue of Cliff was his flight from justice and disappearance in the Tasmanian jungle, where he was unlikely to write his memoirs. The idea of a bestseller by Cliff entitled, *How to be a multimillionaire* made Mr Chimbley's toes curl. His conscience was not crystal clear. He had done badly over the blood and its witnesses. He had done worse by accepting and secreting ill-gotten gains. And now he had vaguely persuaded his colleagues that all was just about in order. If more Shadrach money came his way, could he trust himself to deal with it honestly and discreetly?

It arrived, another load of it, and he postponed the insertion of his advertisement in newspapers.

He was spared the trouble. The receptionist at Chimbley Chimbley and Davis entered his office one morning and spoke to him in an agitated manner.

'Please speak more slowly, Doris,' he said.

Doris was trying to say that three people were in the waiting-room, a mother and daughter and a big angry man.

'What do they want?'

'It's you, sir – they've come for the money.'

'What money? The Shadrach money?'

'The women keep on telling the man he must see you, and he's telling them to shut up in awful language.'

'Are they respectable?'

'They're rough, sir.'

'I'd better have a look at them.'

'Thank you – they were cutting up in reception.'

After a pause the man appeared. He seemed to do so unwillingly, he stood in the open doorway, and women's voices were telling him to 'Go on, go in!' He was middle-aged, red-faced, bristly, and wore shabby dark clothing and an open-necked shirt.

'Morning,' he at last shouted at Mr Chimbley.

'Come in, sir.'

He slammed the door shut and exclaimed under his breath, 'Oh those blasted women!'

'Would you like to sit down, sir?'

His response was to say in his loud voice: 'You've put adverts in papers, haven't you?'

'Sometimes, not recently.'

'Going back a bit?'

'Which advertisements do you mean?'

'Yockenthwaite ones.'

'Oh yes?'

'I'm Yockenthwaite. What's in it for me?'

'If you could prove you are a member of that family, for instance by DNA, you might hear something to your advantage.'

'Money, is that it?'

'I don't have to answer your question, and I won't answer until you speak more politely.'

'I'm not posh.'

'No – you're rude.'

'Look, I don't hold with money for nowt, class money, I'm working class, I'm a working man.'

'You don't have to take the money, you could give it away.'

'So you've got it, have you?'

'I cannot say until I know for sure if you're eligible to receive a possible legacy.'

'Well, if you've got it, and I'm able to get it, that's end of story. Has to be, with my old woman and daughter. They'd string me up to the lamp post if I said no thanks.'

'What is your name, sir, and do you have any serious proof to support your claim?'

'I've proof enough – not that I care one way or t'other – it's for them I'm here – they've been on at it till I said yes.'

'What is your proof, and where is it?'

He patted a side-pocket of his outsize jacket, and replied: 'My grand-nan was Shadrach's aunt.'

'I don't know your name or address.'

'Shilcott, Bert, Albert to you, I shouldn't wonder, and we live over Donning way.'

'Thank you, sir. What are these proofs?'

'Yes, sir, no, sir, three bags full, sir!'

'Mr Shilcott...'

'Okay, you do things as you please, and I'll do 'em straight. I've got certificates.'

'Certificates of what?'

'Grand-nan's marriage lines to my granddad

Harry Shilcott. Miss Susan Yockenthwaite she was. Certificates from there on – birth of my father, birth of me, Susan's savings book, and her death registration. Then there's my parents' proofs.'

'Would you show me?'

'Could take time to study.'

'I'll only take a minute or two.'

By this time the man was sweating. He reached into one pocket, produced a red cotton handkerchief and dried his face and neck as if he had washed them. Reaching into an internal pocket, so-called poacher's pocket, he produced a bundle of papers wrapped in transparent plastic and slapped it down on the desk-top.

Mr Chimbley unpacked them and read rapidly, flicking from one to the next. The silence was only broken by Mr Shilcott's breathing.

'These are sufficient proof.'

Mr Shilcott spoke louder still.

'Course they are – I told you.'

'Mr Shilcott,' Mr Chimbley said. 'I am now willing to offer you confidential information of a monetary nature. Are you, or are you not, ready to receive such information, or would you prefer to leave my office without more ado? I ask because of remarks you have made, indicating your reluctance to accept money.'

'How much is it?'

'Mr Shilcott, a "straight" answer, as you would no doubt call it, please!'

'Missis wanting a new this and that, and our Peggy with her tongue hanging out for cash, how can I stand up and say no?'

'Your problem, sir.'

'Call me Bert. Oh well, a few thousand wouldn't make too much difference.'

'It's not thousands.'

'Blimey! I'll never raise my head. What's the damage?'

'Mr Shilcott, you will be the seventh person to whom I entrust a share of the fortune of Shadrach Yockenthwaite. Shadrach won the money in a lottery, it was never "posh". Perhaps I should warn you that Shadrach's legacies have caused considerable problems.'

'How much?'

'Over five millions.'

'Oh no – oh God – that's done it! Oh Crippen – oh hell! What is it, what have you said to me?'

'Between five and six million pounds, and that's not all. You also inherit Goose Farm, a house with five bedrooms, outbuildings and some acres of land.'

'It's too much.'

'That is not my fault.'

'What? No. Pardon! It's my life, see – you've turned my life work into a waste of time. I'm socialist, born and bred in the politics of the poor people, I'm against wealth, I hate it, I've preached that it ought to be confiscated and spread around equally. I've banged the drum for equality for years and years, and now Lady Luck's punishing me for it.'

'The majority wouldn't have sympathy for the line you're taking. The poor people would change places with you eagerly.'

'That's as may be. But I've been a union man since I was seventeen. Trade Unions, Labour Party, socialism, communism even, they've been my religion. And I've made sacrifices for them, I have! My wife Paula, and our kids, Peggy and Thomas, they don't see things my way, they're not political. Paula wishes I wouldn't work with the tools, she'd like me in a white-collar job and not paying my membership of the Working Men's Club. She's got her ambitions, and they're different from mine. I haven't budged, I've stood my ground, and borne with all the nagging and ragging. Now, now you've played into their hands. If I'm rich, how can I let them be poor? How can I pretend to be poor myself?'

'I'm afraid I see no reason to apologise to you.'

'They'll be geeing themselves up in the waiting room out there, waiting to pounce on me. I never thought of having to defend myself for being a millionaire. I'm knocked flat, I am! What's the next move?'

'I take it you're accepting your inheritance?'

'They'd kill me if I didn't.'

'You could see Mr Burns, manager of the bank that has the money. I could arrange an interview in a private room at the bank.'

'What'll he tell me? I've savings in the Post Office, a few hundred. I've spent what I earned, and paid my National Insurance so that the NHS and Social Service can look after me when I'm old. Where do I start with Mr Burns?'

'He'll help you. Your money will have to be invested, the money that's left after deductions.'

'Half a mo! I've never liked talk of deductions. What are you getting at?'

'Inheritance tax will have to be paid, death duty, at forty per cent.'

'No! Forty per cent of six million's about two and a half million. I can do my mental arithmetic, although I've never needed to, and don't fancy your figures.'

'Tax may be a new experience to you, but some of us live with it day in and day out in one form or another, and I don't think you should be too shocked, considering that taxes are so high largely because of the sort of politics you embrace.'

'So what's my net inheritance?'

'You might have four million clear.'

'Still too much.'

'If that's what you think, it's contrary of you to quibble over having to give a fraction of your wealth to the government.'

'Okay – you were saying – investments will have to be made?'

'Yes, and accounts opened for your dividends to be paid into.'

'You mean money made while I'm sleeping?'

'If you like to put it in that way.'

'I put it like that when I was speechifying and skinning capitalism and the capitalists.'

'Oh well – you may discuss Goose Farm at the bank and the standing order to pay the wages of Mr Higgins, the caretaker, who lives in accommodation in the former stables.'

'I'm not employing anybody, I'll take care of my property.'

'Mr Higgins has been a faithful servant of Yockenthwaites over many years. Do you mean to sack him and evict him from his home? He's old, and he might be surprised to be treated so harshly by a practising socialist.'

'Hold hard! You're tying me in knots. I'll get out of here and try to adjust. I suppose I should thank you.'

'When shall I send our note of fee, Bert?'

'What's that?'

'Our bill for services.'

'But you haven't done services, apart from this chat.'

'Our note of fee will list everything we have done and the time it took to do it.'

'Don't you suck my blood!'

'Good day, sir.'

The two men parted without a handshake; but Mr Chimbley had opened the door for Bert Shilcott and stood by it when Mrs Shilcott and Peggy Shilcott flapped out of the waiting room. They were like birds of prey. The shrieked and squawked and assaulted him with questions and scratching hands.

Albert Shilcott was down to earth, he did not mince matters, was common and proud of it; he was also a muddled idealist, a secret dreamer, a pie-in-the-sky person, a religious atheist, and refused to see the nose on his face. He was no more complicated than other men. He had made as many mistakes as a king in a castle. His attitude to money had always been a kind of contortionism.

He was born and bred up north. His parents were hard people living hard lives tilling other people's land. Bert was precociously a tough guy, then opted for the soft climate of the south, the railways, Track Maintenance, the physical side of it, nothing to do with electrics. He was industrious, he was soon political he swallowed socialism hook, line and sinker. He courted Paula Nettlesmith because she was so dainty, she agreed to marry him because he convinced her that he would be a Member of Parliament. But two babies blocked the road to Westminster.

Not only Peggy and Tom blocked the Shilcotts' way ahead. When Paula was pregnant with Tom she changed the marital double-bed for twins, and soon Bert was sleeping in the attic because he snored. Paula, unsubdued by sex, carried daintiness to discontented lengths, and hen-pecked for every reason and for none. She developed into a handsome dark-haired woman with the flashing eye of envy and rage; and he swelled up and with his jowls and beer-belly looked even more like a bull-frog. She scorned her low-paid hubby and sneered at his socialism, and he stayed later at his Working Men's Club. She kept her cooperation with Bert to a minimum, and he grinned and bore it, hated and feared her, and consoled himself in the company of his powerful union barons and brothers.

Incompatibility reigned at 11 Dean's Drive, their dilapidated home in a down-at-heel terrace.

The marriage was unhappy, and inescapable. The cause was, in one word applicable to both conditions, money. Bert would not or could not earn more of it, and was close into the bargain. Paula had a job in a beauty shop before marriage, after it she was exclusively a mother, she said she needed to be, she was absolutely determined not to sink to being a working wife. And of course the children were open drains in the financial context.

Rows were frequent, and gravitated from being flirty requests for housekeeping cash, to demands with swear words thrown in, to bitter slanging matches including personal remarks of an intimate nature.

Oddly enough, the Yockenthwaite link had been one of the bones of contention even before Shadrach died. Although Bert believed he was fighting the class war, he was not above pandering to Paula's snobbery while he was courting her. He dropped the name and lived to regret it.

'They sound like interesting people,' Paula remarked.

'I don't know them personally.'

'What's that name you mentioned?'

'Shadrach – it's out of the Bible.'

'Were they churchy?'

'Not likely – Shadrach was farm labour – and cows have to be milked on Sundays too.'

Paula never laughed at Bert's jokes.

'But he got the farm in the end, he inherited, didn't he?'

'So they say. Goose Farm, it's called.'

'It must be worth money.'

'Could be.'

'Why don't you look him up, Bert?'

'We won't get anything out of Shadrach, he was known for being mean.'

'But he'll be old, and he's got no children.'

'I'm not after dead men's shoes, I'm not begging nobody.'

'You don't know which side your bread's buttered, do you?'

'Leave off! I've never met the man. He'd see through me. And I won't go cap in hand.'

All this, the lack of money in the Shilcott home, the rich relation untapped, was like the tinder, and Mr Chimbley's advertisements were the sparks.

Paula saw several. She sometimes bought a posh paper and her eye was caught by the name in the Personal columns. She was not slow to use the ads against her husband.

'Shadrach must have died, and we never knew him,' she remarked.

'Well, I'm not crying,' he retorted. 'He never had no money, and they said Goose Farm was a broken-down place.'

'Answer the advert, Bert, or I will.'

'You're not a Yockenthwaite, not by a long chalk. Mind your business, will you!'

Paula enlisted the children in her treasure-hunt.

'Peggy needs a new bike. Tom's grown out of his school uniform. Who's paying, Bert?'

Peggy whined: 'Oh Daddy, why do we have

to be poor?' And Tom grumbled: 'Boys at school laugh at me because my clothes don't fit.'

'You only have to give that solicitor a ring,' Paula said repeatedly.

'Don't you nag me! ... What makes you think old Shadrach had money? ... If we got Goose Farm, we'd be landed, we'd be bloody capitalists ... I'm not moving house for no one ... Shut your traps, you kids, you're spoilt enough by your mother,' Bert batted back at different times.

His mind was changed by the health scare. He had a heart spasm – not quite a heart attack – at the Working Men's Club one evening. He was carried away in an ambulance, had tests in hospital, was put on pills against cholesterol and to lower blood pressure, and returned to Dean's Drive chastened.

He was working things out logically for a change. The trouble with his ticker was attributable to his home life rather than to any constitutional weakness. He had stayed too late at the club, drunk too much beer, had too many political arguments, and exhausted himself: why? Because he was giving the missis a wide berth. He was driven out of Dean's Drive by a dainty girl who had turned into a beast of a woman – she could be the death of him. The alternative consequences were to divorce her, but he rejected that idea, he cared for his kids, he would not do what the rich folk do; or else to keep quiet for as long as he could bear to live with her. Quietness would be obtainable in only one way, by stuffing all the open mouths with money, and by not picking and choosing where the money came from.

He boasted of his principles, as people do who have the elastic type. He was Treasurer of the Christmas Club at the WMC, and he had borrowed from it now and again. He put the money back, nobody noticed, no harm done – flexibility was not a crime. Better to bend before his family's opposition than to break, he gradually came round to thinking.

He ventured into the cloud-cuckoo-land of what he could do with a few hundred extra pounds. They could buy him not necessarily love, but at least more respect. He could give it to socialism, which was always begging for other people's money. It might raise him up into a position of authority, or get him sent on so-called 'fact-finding' missions to the South of France or Miami.

A pinch of cynicism forced the issue. He faced the fact that many of his socialist heroes were moneyed men, had private means, were expensively educated, and money-grubbers: why not take a step or two along a well-trodden path? He thought of no more than a few steps: an inheritance measured in pockets-full. It would not relieve him of the need to work, or steal from him the pride he took in being one of the workers of the world, a have-not, a foot-soldier of the army of the masses marching towards revolution and revenge.

So it was that he got a sicknote and a day off, and spent incredibly valuable time with Mr Chimbley.

Paula had insisted on keeping him company – or was it an eye on him? – and Peggy would not be left out. Peggy was called Piggy at school: aged fifteen she was overweight. She was also bossy and sure of herself, although she was said to be shy underneath. Tom, the big baby of the family, had exams at school. He thought it was unfair that he was not allowed to wait to hear good news with his mummy and sis. He too was overweight, built like his father, and as materialistic as his mother.

Paula and Peggy set upon Bert with unladylike cries when he was leaving the premises at Chimbley Chimbley and Davis. Outside in the street he told them to get in the car, he was not saying nothing for all to hear. They hurried along to where the old Ford was parked and piled in fast. As the doors slammed Bert spoke.

'It's a million.'

Three words quelled the noise and brought about silence, almost holy, and temporary.

Paula burst into tears. Peggy began to bawl out her 'I wants'. Bert admitted he was gobsmacked over and over again. He dwelt on the mystery of Shadrach's wealth: how exactly was it won, how does a miser win anything? He drove back home – he was not going to meet Mr Burns with his wife and daughter in tow, listening to figures being bandied about that revealed more money than they would know. Tom was fetched early from school, and the children and their mother busied themselves with calculators.

Bert slipped away. He sneaked – he felt he

was sneaking – to the NatWest. He was intent on concealing money from his family in particular and the world in general. He talked with Mr Burns in a private office, and it was agreed that one million should be placed in a new account with cheque book, interest-bearing and in his name. The rest of his money was to be in a second account, again in his name, but without cheque book and never sending him statements – he would see statements when he was in the bank. The household account, old-established and in the Shilcotts' joint names, would function as before, receiving Bert's wages and providing for household expenditure.

On the way home he stopped for a drink at the WMC, but no other members were there, they were either working or having afternoon naps, and he continued to Dean's Drive, which suddenly looked squalid to a millionaire.

The Shilcotts were accustomed to big breakfasts and not much to eat until tea, a meat tea at six o'clock-ish. Paula and the children had cooked a surprise for Bert while he was absent: they were giving him a dinner out to celebrate their financial transformation. He did not like the idea, but could not very well object. He was being treated with approval instead of scorn: how could he complain? But he sussed the why and the wherefore, and did not like phony affection any more than rudeness and exasperation.

At seven o'clock he was blind-folded. Paula drove the family into the town centre, and the children led Bert into a warm place and removed the scarf covering his eyes. They were in a restaurant, the best restaurant, Galto's by name, and a man in a dinner jacket was leading them to a table for four near a dance floor. Bert was uneasy: he had spoken out publicly against the prices Galto charged for food. He read the menu with pain in the region of his heart; he had to let the others order the meal and a bottle of wine costing as much as his wage for a week. He protested faintly, but was told to lie back and enjoy it: they had the money, he was not to be a mangy spoilsport. He ate with difficulty, he had to ask for beer to enable him to swallow those mouthfuls of money. He was not surprised to receive the bill, his surprise was that he could bear to write a cheque which almost used up the balance of cash in the household account.

Then he was hailed by another diner. Mr Norton was passing by with a party of people. Mr Norton was the managing director of the rail transport area. He was Bert's boss and he recognised Bert and cracked a joke and everybody laughed.

The joke was: 'Hullo there, Bert, you must have robbed a bank!'

The price of Bert's money stuck in his throat. His 'straight' character, personality, attitudes and conduct were being twisted out of true. It was bad enough when only Mr Chimbley and he himself had known how rich he had become, but now it was family, Mr Burns, Mr Norton, neighbours, shopkeepers, Tom, Dick and Harry. He had been so hard on the hypocrisy rife in modern society, and so down on champagne socialism, that he was called a hypocrite at work. Why was he working, why steal another man's job, when he could afford to cruise round the world or put his feet up in his fancy farmhouse? Somebody at the Working Men's Club used the word Judas, and Lee Flowers, a friend of his, accused him of defecting to the bosses' side. Bert had not been slow to foresee difficulties: he had been such a high-profile activist for underdogs that his switch into top dog was bound to cause comment. But the comments were sharper than expected, and the envy and jealousy crueller.

Gone were his popular progressions in the High Street, his loud-hailing of friends and acquaintances, his unspoken statement that he was poor but proud, an English commoner who was also a king in his modest way. Now he walked humbly and without raising his voice, pretending not to be as rich as he was. He avoided gatherings of adults and made detours round gangs of schoolboys. Without losing much weight, he was a shadow of his former self.

And home was not his castle. His wife and children were not content to wag their tongues out of doors, they nagged him non-stop. They staked their claims to some of the 'million' pounds, and they felt they would get more the more they were arrogant and obstreperous. Paula had insisted on herself and the children having one hundred thousand pounds apiece. She harped on at least that division of the spoils, and she and Peggy and Tom all wanted Bert to go and transfer such sums into three personal bank accounts. When he delayed, saying he would have to see about the tax implications, Paula said and the children implied that they expected to get the money tax free – he could pay whatever tax was owed and not bother them about it.

The move into Goose Farm had multiplied difficulties for Bert. It raised him more steps up the social ladder. It was out of town, he had to drive his people to school and shops, and he realised he could no longer carry on with his job. He gave in his notice on a bitter day, when he had felt honour bound to sack Mr Higgins: he almost cried twice over, what were he and his world coming to?

Paula engaged builders, interior decorators, curtain and carpet people, and gardeners, to make the place fit for her to live in, and their estimates terrified the man who would have to pay the bills. Peggy and Tom were bored by the country and harassed their father non-stop: 'Can we have a car of our own – or motorbike – will you drive us in to the cinema – where's our money, we'd go up to London if we had it – when will you see Mr Burns?'

Peggy and Tom created a row in which both their parents were involved.

'Dad, have you made a will?' Peggy asked, and Tom stirred the pot. He chimed in: 'If you don't make a will, all your money goes to Mum.'

Eventually Bert made appointments and drove

into town by himself. He left his country house and was to spend time with his solicitor and banker, like a proper gentleman. In Mr Chimbley's office he ascertained that his taxes were all paid and gave instructions about a will. He then crossed the road to talk to Mr Burns. He transferred three sums of one hundred thousand pounds from his 'million' pounds into new personal accounts in the names of Paula, Peggy and Tom. He felt quite ill when he realised he was running through nearly half a million, but was revived by the sight of a statement of his secret account – there were so many figures that he could not read them, and each one seemed to him a blessing.

He returned to Goose Farm with the personal cheque books for three. He was thanked but grudgingly. Paula pointed out that she had a hundred thousand in her account, and the two children ditto, whereas, judging by the information he had given them, there must be five hundred getting on for six hundred thousand pounds in the household account. Was that his idea of fair play? It was selfish in her book – he was a scrooge to his children.

Bert was on the slippery slope of being rich beyond his dreams, and was unhappier than ever before. He had nothing to do, he was ashamed of his leisure, and he had dilemmas. How was he to divide his estate more fairly, yet without leaving too much to persons who did not deserve it? His politer exchanges with his wife were like armed ceasefires in a battle, and his children only spoke to him about money, his, which they wanted more of.

A full-scale family row seemed to be an end-all, but was the opposite.

The men working in the house brought bills from head offices, and Bert looked at them over his breakfast egg and bacon. Paula, Peggy and Tom watched and saw that his temperature was rising.

He chucked the bills at Paula and said she could pay them.

She said: 'That I will not! This is your house and you'll pay for maintenance and improvements. You've got more money than the rest of us put together.'

'I'm holding on to money to feed us,' he replied. 'You'll fritter what's yours, what I've given you. I'll hold back for my old age.'

'You're old now, Bert, you are, and you've made no provision for my future or your children's. I'm not spending my money on your property. You make your will, and we'll see.'

Peggy put her oar in.

'I couldn't buy a decent house with what you've given me, Dad. I thought you'd be more generous.'

And Tom said: 'If you don't make your will, Dad, I'll go to the solicitor and get to the bottom of where the money's gone.'

'Don't you threaten me, boy. Don't any of you dare! You'll be sorry if you do.'

'What's that?' Paula pounced on his hint. 'Is there money you're keeping back? Is there more money?'

'No. That's the wrong tree to bark up. Stop your narking! I'm sick of the lot of you!'

He strode out of the kitchen.

Paula shouted after him: 'You're wasting your breakfast, spendthrift!'

Bert drove away. He drove dangerously, his sight blurred, not knowing where he was going. In the middle of the morning he drew up in a lay-by and spent time between weeping and sleep. Then he turned the car for home, his new home, Goose Farm.

He walked in and called Paula by name. He meant to patch things up for the time being. The workmen were hammering and sawing, and one of them pointed upwards. He climbed the stairs, pushed upon the door of Paula's bedroom and looked in. She was on the floor with the paper-hanger, William by name. They were on the floor, amongst the gummy offcuts, behind the bed, and copulating. They struggled to their feet, Bert approached, Paula stood in front of William defensively. Bert handed her off and felled him with a blow to the head, blood flowed, and Bert stormed out and back into the car.

He spent the day and part of the night at the Working Men's Club. He was past caring that he was richer than his cronies there, he bought drinks for everyone and laughed at his money – most of it was gone, he said, and good riddance too! He got drunk, he had a sleep in the car before he hoped he could reach Goose Farm safely, and he entered the house without waking anyone to his knowledge, and passed out in his bedroom.

He woke at eleven the next morning. He was unwell, and still more miserable to think about yesterday and that his late rising today had apparently caused no concern. He washed, dressed and went downstairs. He found Paula sitting in the lounge with a piece of plaster across her cheek and the corner of her mouth.

'What's wrong with you?' he asked.

'It's covering the place you hit me,' she said.

'I never hit you.'

'Really? I have witnesses.'

'Where are the workmen?'

'They've walked off the job because of what you did to William.'

'It's what William did to you and me they should have objected to.'

'They don't see it like that.'

'They're ignorant.'

'Are they indeed? I thought that was what you are.'

'Where are the children, Paula?'

'Gone to London for good.'

'They can't.'

'Why not? They've two hundred thousand pounds between them. We're not being pushed around and treated shabby by you any more.'

'Me, push you around? Try again!'

'I'm suing you for divorce. I've instructed a solicitor of my own. I'll take half of every single thing you've got, money, property. That's the law. And you won't stand a chance against us because of your violence.'

'Is that so?'

'Yes it is.'

'No,' he contradicted.

He left her, and drove into town. He had not said goodbye, he had dodged out through the side door. He called on Mr Burns, carrying a big old suitcase. In Mr Burns' office he asked for the money in his household account and in his secret account, a sum in the region of three millions, to be packed in notes in the case as quickly as possible. Mr Burns objected, saying he had performed a similar task for the late Mr Wayne Yockenthwaite, and hoping that Mr Bert Yockenthwaite was not bent on any drastic or irreparable action. Bert told him to 'shut it', and Mr Burns said the case would be ready for collection by four o'clock in the afternoon.

Mr Burns and several bank clerks saw Bert at four. At ten o'clock that evening Paula Shilcott rang the police. The police rang Mr Chimbley, who knew nothing; but Mr Chimbley rang Mr Burns, and they jumped to conclusions. The body was found the next morning, in Teasham Tunnel, on the railway line, electrocuted. Apparently a ticket officer had noticed a man he thought he recognised, a worker in the Maintenance Unit, walking into the tunnel without his regulation yellow coat, and had thought it a bit funny.

Time passed, and in the private residence of the Morgan Chimbleys, in the bedroom they shared, the Yockenthwaites were again the subject of their intimate conversation.

Heather said: 'It makes me so sad to think of all that money going to waste.'

203

Morgan commented: 'The Yockenthwaites are not even any good at being miserly.' And he sounded a Churchillian note: 'I've never heard of so many members of the same family losing so much money in such a short space of time.'

'They must have very bad values.'

'No doubt.'

'Will there be more money to come?'

'Possibly - according to my reckoning, yes - I live in hopes - but we must remember that Paula Shilcott and the children are the rightful heirs of more of Shadrach's money, should any materialise.'

Several more months elapsed.

One evening, as the Chimbleys were getting ready for bed, Morgan cleared his throat and said: 'I have spoken to Mr Burns, Heather. We were discussing the Shilcott problem. Apparently Mr Shilcott gave the members of this family one hundred thousand pounds apiece, and, as we know, Paula Shilcott, Peggy and Tom, after Bert's funeral, decamped in a rush to London and then to the USA. And they spent the money, all of it, in their three accounts.'

'I cannot be sorry for them, Morgan. A hundred thousand is not to be sneezed at.'

'That is not the point, Heather. The Shilcotts have vanished. Nobody knows where they are or what has happened to them. They have been missing for an appreciable time now.'

'Are they dead, dear?'

'Mr Burns was suggesting that we could assume so.'

'Does that mean what I think it means?'

'If those Yockenthwaites were legally established to be non-existent, they will have forfeited their chances to inherit from Shadrach.'

'Who would the money belong to?'

'That's the point.'

'Could we keep it?'

'If it should be unclaimed, maybe.'

'Is "maybe" more positive than "possibly"?'

'Could there be another claimant? I doubt it.'

'How much might it be?'

'Millions again.'

'Oh, Morgan, how I love you.'

'Yes - well - thank you. Incidentally, the suitcase containing most of the Shilcott money has never been found. Some rogue must have pinched it.'

Ninth Chapter of Nine

Both Morgan Chimbleys, but especially Heather, suffered emotional trauma in the fullness of time in connection with Yockenthwaites.

More of Shadrach's money had arrived, twelve millions, no less, from the Antilles. By this time, the heirs of Bert were out of the running, they were legally disinherited by being as good as dead. Chimbley, Chimbley and Davis received the money in cheque form, and it could belong to Morgan, who had acted for the owner of the seventy-plus millions throughout. Excitement reigned in the hearts of the two most interested parties. Morgan tried in vain to check and suppress it.

'The money is not ours yet, Heather.'

'But I've already spent it, supposing, Morgan.'

'A genuine heir may clamber out of the woodwork, as others did.'

'But there can't be more Yockenthwaites, there can't be any more people as feckless as the others.'

'I tend to agree.'

'How much could we be getting, just in theory?'

'Seven million net – hypothetically, of course.'

'But hypothetical's fun, Morgan! What a lot of good we could do with seven million! We'd be the richest people in Teasham.'

Morgan Chimbley's cautionary tales were not completely 'efficacious', as he once revealed to his Heather. He too dallied with the notion of early retirement and cruises on luxury ships.

But an envelope landed on his desk, small, brown, on thin paper, and the letter inside was short and written on paper with lines. The writer was a Miss Gloria Thwaite, and she actually lived in Teasham, in a cottage in a back street, Pike Passage. She was staking her claim, and she was deeply disappointing the Chimbleys.

Morgan broke the news to Heather by telephone – he was breaking with custom as well.

She said: 'Can't you tear the letter up?'

'No.'

'Why not?'

'She'll call – she lives ten minutes from the office.'

'You're so honest, Morgan.'

'I'm sorry, dear.'

Miss Thwaite's phraseology was a deterrent to doing something dishonest.

She asked if there was 'money knocking about for natives of the Yockenthwaite tribe': a self-confident and upper class stylistic flourish. How could any relation of Shadrach be upper class? But Morgan knew enough to know that a female of that class could be a law unto herself, highfalutin and unpredictable, and that it was a mistake for solicitors to tangle with such persons. He thought of having a word with Mr Burns, but decided not to. He was afraid Mr Burns would never be in favour of Chimbley Chimbley and Davis pocketing so much of Shadrach's money. A worst case scenario would be that Mr Burns was friendly with Miss Thwaite and might appropriate the windfall and guide it in her direction.

He rang the telephone number on the writing paper.

A high-pitched voice, between forceful and musical, came on the line.

'Is that Miss Thwaite?' he inquired.

'Yes. Who are you?'

'I'm Chimbley of Chimbley Chimbley and Davis.'

She asked: 'Which Chimbley are you?'

'I'm the one in the middle, Morgan Chimbley.'

'How uncomfortable!'

'Excuse me?'

'You must have received my letter, Mr Chimbley?'

'I have, I have it here.'

'You've advertised for Yockenthwaites, and I've considered an application for some years.'

'Why did you not apply, Miss Thwaite?'

'I didn't want to hear anything to my advantage. I've been lucky, and didn't want to do anybody down.'

'That is a praiseworthy sentiment.'

'Oh I'm not sentimental, I'm a realist.'

'What changed your mind?'

'Yes, well, I've been concerned for Mr Higgins, who was caretaker at Goose Farm. Do you know what I'm talking about?'

'I think I do.'

'He wasn't treated well, and I was hoping to repair the damage.'

'Explanations might be in order, Miss Thwaite. Would you permit me to call on you?'

'Please do, Mr Chimbley. I'm not often called upon by solicitors. A new experience is often delightful. Would tea today suit you?'

'Thank you, yes.'

'Four-thirty?'

'Until then!'

He could not help liking her. He approved of her, in spite of himself. He knew in his bones that she was not like Cliff Macdonald. He did not automatically grudge her the large extra slice of luck that might be hers. He was interested to meet her.

Pike Passage was a terrace of probably Edwardian houses, each comprising basement, ground and first floor, with small front gardens, facing south. Opposite, on the other side of the road, larger and later semi-detached houses looked north. Cars were parked in and out of garages and carports. Through traffic was absent. Quiet respectability seemed to reign.

Miss Thwaite appeared in the doorway of The Wedge. She limped, she was crooked, she walked with difficulty, but bravely, smiling. She had sharp twinkling blue eyes, wavy white hair, her head was a size too big for her body, and her ready laughter had a kind of gurgle in it.

They sat in her sitting-room, in armchairs on either side of a coal fire in an iron grate, and the teapot was warming on a purpose-built projection.

'Miss Thwaite,' Mr Chimbley began, 'before

210

we go any further, may I ask if you are a blood relative of the Yockenthwaite family?'

She was, she said. Her father had dropped the 'Yocken' since it meant oxen, and he owned none. No, she had not known Shadrach; but he had been considered a black sheep by his Yockenthwaite contemporaries, a grumpy poor relation in his lifetime, who had died with largesse to scatter – witness Mr Chimbley's advertisements. She had heard in roundabout ways of the bad luck of his beneficiaries. Her branch of the family had been land agents up north, of whom she was the sole survivor. She was not exactly after Shadrach's money, she had merely wondered if loot was going begging.

A few letters, books, yellowing photographs and means of identification convinced Mr Chimbley that he could speak thus: 'I have distributed Shadrach's money seven times. He hid it abroad; and it has been repatriated gradually over the last few years. As a rule I insisted on a DNA test before releasing money to a claimant. But I was defrauded once – more to the point, the Yockenthwaites were – by a forgery, and now I prefer to go by my own experience and judgment. I see clearly that you are who you say you are, Miss Thwaite, and therefore I can tell you without more ado that you are an heiress. Yes! No, I am not joking. You have inherited twelve million pounds, gross.'

'I think I had better make our tea,' she said.

'You take my news more calmly than the other heirs.'

'I have no need of the money.'

211

'Even so, your hand didn't shake when you infused the tea.'

'Money can do as much harm as lack of money. What a platitude! How I would hate poor people to hear me say such a thing! Your tea, Mr Chimbley, with milk and sugar?'

'Only milk, thank you.'

'Please cut the walnut cake and help yourself to a slice.'

'Thank you again.'

'I feel it's for me to be thanking you.'

'Not at all. I shall be paid via my firm for bearing you these tidings. My understanding is that the money in question is the final tranche of the winnings of an international sweepstake. I'm glad you will have it. Some of the beneficiaries never benefited from their good luck, and most had bad luck into the bargain. I thought I should explain why you are the eighth beneficiary.'

'What happened to the other seven?'

'They squandered the money, and it drove most of them into graves of one sort and another.'

'What's another sort of grave?'

'In a swimming pool, for instance.'

'An accident?'

'An accident on purpose.'

'Suicide?'

'I fear so.'

'What a pity! Is there a second instance?'

'There was an airline crash. There were doubtful deaths.'

'I don't mean to die doubtfully.'

'Quite right, Miss Thwaite.'

'You said "gross". What is net?'

'I can see you are a businesslike person.'

'Not far wrong, Mr Chimbley! I was my father's book-keeper. I was a businesswoman until my parents died and I came south and retired in The Wedge. I've been blessed, blessed with a sunny temperament, and I got over my handicap many years ago. That's my story in a nutshell.'

'May I help you to a slice of cake, Miss Thwaite?'

'I've been looking forward to it.'

'You asked me a question. What is net? Tax and deductions will probably reduce your inheritance to between six and seven million net.'

'Deductions are for your bill?'

'More or less.'

'Oh Mr Chimbley, I'm sorry – I'm not a "more or less" person, I'm "all or nothing". Now, I realise that I'm going to be busier than ever before, and I would very much like to delegate the management of the fortune that seems to be coming my way. I do not want a stockbroker, I do not want to make money or to lose it. My money should be ready, if you know what I mean. It should be in cash instruments, as I believe they're called – cheque accounts at the bank – easily accessible – and never complex or mysterious. Would you help me? I'd like to trust you. But I'm not a book-keeper for nothing. You'd have to give me details of what you do and have done, and itemised accounts, say on a quarterly basis. Is it a deal?'

'Miss Thwaite, you amaze me.'

'Not an answer, Mr Chimbley.'

He cleared his throat. He had taken an unprofessional fancy to this surprising little lady, and was tempted to do her bidding. At the same time he foresaw complications.

'I am not an accountant, Miss Thwaite,' he said.

'No? Well, I have a friend who was an accountant in the City of London, he'll watch over that side of things.'

'I am unaccustomed to being supervised.'

'Are you rejecting me, Mr Chimbley?'

'No, no, certainly not, nothing of the sort, but I would like to mention the property you also inherit, Goose Farm. The fraudster already mentioned mortgaged Goose Farm to raise capital, and I have had to use Shadrach's money to disencumber the property. Secondly, Shadrach chose to place his money not in conventional interest-bearing bonds, but in cash safe-keeping accounts with dates of surrender. He seems to have been determined not to receive income, and not to pay tax. Anyway, the cash arrived with a minimum of paperwork, therefore I have been unable to guarantee that the money I have distributed, including your inheritance, precisely matches the whole of the sum of money Shadrach won in his lottery. Ready reckoning has had to be my guide, and I apologise for possible inaccuracies.'

'Thank you,' she said. 'Shall we keep accounts from today onwards? And would you like to call me Gloria?'

'Thank you – no – I think not – I would be happier with respectful formality, if you wouldn't mind.'

'Well done, Mr Chimbley, you have passed the first test. Informality's the bane of the age we live in.'

'If it would not tire you, Miss Thwaite, shall we get down to brass tacks?'

'Please, Mr Chimbley.'

The brass tacks that Mr Chimbley and Miss Thwaite got down to were not exclusively about brass. When he had finished talking tax and banking to her, they discovered they had things in common, age – they were both in their seventies – some worldly wisdom, and detachment from the preoccupations of their younger years. She had no noticeable romantic attachment; he, although married to Heather, had never had one. She was financially independent, and he, in truth, had almost skimmed a sufficiency of cream off the milk of other people's money. They were somehow complementary. Gloria Thwaite was a free spirit, whereas Mr Chimbley was in the mould for solicitors. She was cultivated, he was a philistine. She was educated by the two great teachers, pain and reading. She was sensitive, intuitive, charitable and religious; he was nothing like that. She had become what she was by passing stern tests year after year, month after month, even daily, ever since she limped into being a toddler; he had learnt to be what he

215

was by passing an exam in his youth. That the two of them got on well together was basically due to her seeing through him at a glance, having sympathy for his limitations, and realising that he would not try or be able to browbeat her or get in her way.

She was the younger of two children of David Thwaite and Phillis, originally his PA. They were successful in their business, but unlucky in their children. Their son Tony was a sweet dunce, who perished by accident on a school outing to Wales. Their daughter had a spinal defect.

Gloria was soon aware of not being glorious. She was ill, always ill, and undergoing tortures by optimistic doctors. She obviously disappointed her parents, and cost them money they grudged. Her childhood was a nightmare, her youth was nothing but wretchedness for a romantic girl, her middle age was despair; but her older age was miraculous for several reasons, she had reached it, after all; secondly, her parents died; thirdly, her spine decided to have mercy on her; and fourthly, she had a chance to count blessings, that she had lovely friends, she could thank her God for relenting, she had just enough money, and perhaps would be able to make up for lost time.

As soon as her new finances were in order, and her millions in reach of her cheque book, she asked Mr Chimbley to find Mr Higgins and bring him to The Wedge for elevenses one morning. Mr Chimbley warned her that his time was expensive, but she said he would be worth every penny, she needed him to be present, and to take over from where she would have to leave off.

The two visitors duly rang her doorbell. Jack Higgins was an elderly man, white-haired but red cheeked.

'Thank you for coming to see me,' she began, smiling at him and giving Mr Chimbley's arm a grateful squeeze.

'Good morning, miss,' he replied.

'Can you spare me time to have a cup of coffee, Mr Higgins?'

He said he could, and she led the way into her sitting-room.

'Mr Higgins,' she said after they were seated, 'you don't know me, but I know that you were not treated nicely by my very distant relations, Albert and Paula Shilcott. You took care of my family's house, Goose Farm, and they did not appreciate your services over a long period.'

'True, miss,' he admitted, 'but that's an old story.'

'I understand you have no home of your own at present.'

'I'm not a complaining man, miss.'

'The Council have not rehoused you?'

'Not yet, I'm on a waiting list, and I have temporary accommodation.'

'In a church?'

'Under a church, you might say – there are quite a lot of us there.'

'You have no family, Mr Higgins?'

'I lost my wife twenty-three years ago.'

217

'I'm sorry. No children?'

'No, miss. My daughter had the same disease as my wife. I lost both.'

'Would you accept help from me? I would like to compensate for the ingratitude of my relations.'

'It's kind of you, miss, but I'm sure you have many more needy cases to help.'

'There's a flat you could have for life.'

'Pardon?'

'I'm offering you a flat for life, no rent to pay, and all done legally.'

'Oh no, miss...'

'Listen, Mr Higgins! I've come into money unexpectedly. My aim now is to do unexpected things for other people. I'm sane and I'm serious. If you say yes, my solicitor, Mr Chimbley, will make it legal.'

'I'm thunderstruck.'

'What about coffee?'

'You're too kind, miss.'

'You think over my offer while I boil the kettle.'

Some days later Mr Chimbley's attendance was again required. He went along to The Wedge and was given some information. Then the doorbell rang and a young woman, thirtyish, prettily smiling in spite of shadows under her blue eyes, stood on the doorstep.

Gloria Thwaite welcomed her with open arms, kissed her, introduced her to Mr Chimbley, and they moved into the sitting-room and sat round the fire.

'Where are the children?' Gloria asked.

'At school at the moment, touch wood,' Charlotte replied.

'Two, aren't there?'

'Michael and Tommy – they're six and five years old.'

'I know you've been having a rotten time, dear.'

'Gran's told you, I suppose?'

'Your granny's my lifelong friend. Her worries have always been mine, and especially vice versa.'

Charlotte's eyes filled with tears and she said: 'I'm so sorry to be worrying everyone.'

'Not your fault – can't be otherwise – but help is at hand, if wanted.'

'Oh thank you, thank you – but you can't – I'm in too much of a mess – I'll pull myself out of it somehow. Please don't strain your finances on my account.'

Miss Thwaite and Mr Chimbley exchanged a meaningful glance.

'Put me in the picture, will you? Tell me the truth, Charlotte, if you can bear to.'

'You came to my wedding, didn't you?'

'Yes, I enjoyed it.'

Edgar courted me for a year – the wedding was the anniversary of our meeting – he seemed to be a good person, hardworking at whatever he did in financial services, and I thought we were happily married – we had the two children and had bought a house in the country with a garden and trees.'

'He walked out on you?'

219

'There might have been warning signs, he was in London on weekdays and sometimes spent the night there, staying with a colleague – but I didn't suspect anything, I had no reason to – he was not bad at being a husband and a father. One evening he didn't come back. He was late for supper. Then he rang to say bye-bye. That was how he explained what he was doing to us, "bye-bye".'

'Not the end of the story?'

'Far from it! He left us without any money, with bills to pay for our mortgage and water and so on, he used the credit card in our joint names which was linked to our household account. I discovered I owed more than twenty thousand pounds. Bailiffs invaded our home and took away furniture. Edgar still won't allow me even to try to sell the house – somebody's said he's still borrowing money against its value. The Social Services have been as good as possible, but ... but my children and I, we're a lost cause.'

She cried with her head in her hands.

Gloria said: 'Your granny sent you here for advice. Your granny's a little behind the times – I haven't given her all my news. I'll get you out of prison.'

'What?'

'I'll rescue you financially.'

'Oh, you can't – you couldn't – and I wouldn't have pleaded poverty if I'd known you'd think I was asking for money.'

'You must go and talk to my friend and solicitor, Mr Chimbley. He'll pay your debt and extricate you from your house and provide for you to be free.'

'Oh, why? Why and how? '

'I needed help in order to survive, for better or for worse. Now I'm suddenly by chance, by accident, in a position to do the helping. Don't ask me "why" too often – if you do, I'll preach. No preaching, no telling you what's done and what not to do, no judging. But I'll let you into a secret. For you, dear, I'd like to remedy the mistake that I might have made if I'd had your advantages. There! Go to the bank with Mr Chimbley – I rather think time shouldn't be wasted.'

Charlotte cried and kissed her benefactor, and did as she was told. In days that came and went, other people sat in the chair in which she was given that best of all boons, a second chance. Old friends had their far-fetched dreams realised, the improbable made possible, and pain eased. Young people were rescued and encouraged. Opportunities, education, were offered round like sweets in a paper bag. How many tears not of sorrow but relief, of hope renewed, of revised opinions of the character of mankind, which had seemed to be callous and uncaring, were shed in The Wedge? Gloria's funds of good cheer were apparently fathomless.

But, of course, they also attracted the attention of Mr Chimbley and Mr Burns. Grave questions were raised about Gloria running through her fortune. The spectre of penury was summoned to the feast. Now urgent business meetings were arranged, and in the sitting-room of The Wedge elevenses were served while the bank statements, letters from the Inland Revenue, surveyors' reports on Goose Farm, and estimates of liabilities were laid out on the coffee table.

'Mr Burns, you have tea, don't you?' Gloria asked. 'But I've forgotten, are you a milk and sugar man?'

And she said to Mr Chimbley: 'I know you prefer coffee in the morning? You only like tea at teatime.'

When such questions were settled, the businessmen tried to be businesslike.

Mr Chimbley said: 'Getting on for a year has elapsed since I announced that you had inherited a fortune. Tax has been paid on the principal, but more tax, gift tax, will no doubt be levied on your expenditure to date. Your generosity is commendable. I would just warn that governments in general do not approve of financial kindness between persons. We may have more trouble with the Inland Revenue.'

'What's the bill?'

'No bill yet, Miss Thwaite, but we need to be prepared.'

'Oh well – sufficient unto the day is the evil thereof.'

Mr Burns chipped in.

'Miss Thwaite, your outgoings in these last months have exceeded the million pounds mark. In a similar period before the arrival of so much money, you had seven hundred and ten pounds approximately. May I suggest that your expenses have increased dramatically?'

'I know, and it's nice to know.'

'Very true, but...'

'Oh Mr Burns, let no "but" come between us! I am not on the rocks, so why the Mayday calls? Can I press you to a Hobnob, gentlemen?'

They had the grace to laugh. They all laughed, the gentlemen because they liked to be twisted round a tiny female little finger, and the lady for fun.

Mr Chimbley attempted to recall them to an outstanding matter.

'Goose Farm, Miss Thwaite, I'm aware that you don't care for the black weathervane, but have you decided what to do with the property?'

'Not yet,' she echoed him, and they had another laugh.

Time marched on, and Gloria Thwaite kept up with it as best she could, thinner maybe, but continuing to do favours to deserving cases, a hip or a denture here, a holiday there, central heating somewhere else, and always monetary contributions towards living expenses. Her charity was personal and homely, never used to interfere in a controversy or to force an issue. She tried to be fair, although she would say that the only totally fair manifestation of life on earth was death. When the recipients of her bounty spoke of their luck, she would reply: 'What about mine?' She had always had a better brain than body, and now her speculative thinking pondered the phenomenal aspects of money, her millions and the psychological impacts of having too little and too much. She was ready to discuss the subject open-mindedly: she startled people by asking them why they thought she had struck gold without investment or effort.

Her own analyses were delivered piecemeal, but amounted to quite a treatise.

'Chance rules the world,' she said. 'People who say they made their luck, and we can all do so if we make the effort, are arrogant and stupid. They talk like that because they happen to have had a lucky break. Success and failure are beyond our control, although you can or you can't cash in on a success, and you can or you can't rise above failure and poverty. Who gives us chances? Atheism's answer is so awful – that we're responsible and to blame for everything. I prefer to believe in miracles. Religion's much more comfortable to live with than atheism, egoism, politicians' whims and the NHS.'

Gloria had picked up details of those with whom Shadrach had played the game of God.

'They seem to have been undone by his money,' she remarked. 'He was a mean man, you know, and must have invested his money so as to fool the taxman and not contribute to the common weal. He never spent any of his winnings, according to his bank manager – and perished before he had started to enjoy them. He forgot that luck cuts both ways. He left no will. My solicitor and his, Mr Chimbley, distributed chunks of his wealth as they turned up, and every kind of the fates reserved for rich people afflicted my seven predecessors in one way or another. I don't want to criticise, I'm not smug, only grateful that I haven't been squashed flat by the weight of my millions.'

She corrected the statement above.

'I can't boast that money out of the blue wasn't a shock to my system. It shocked me, I wasn't above being flabbergasted. Talk about the change of life! My life's changed twice, and I'm not even dead yet. But I hadn't been starving when I got the money – none of the other heirs were actually starving, I gather – in an ideal world we should have been able to cope with having money to burn. Unfortunately, what was not fortunate, was the age we live in – so materialistic, no room for the spirit, no time for the inner life. Not many people read nowadays. I wish they read Kipling, his poem *If* in particular. Kipling wrote that we should learn to be resistant equally to good and bad experience. He knew what he was talking about, he never got over the loss of his only son in the 1914 war. New riches mean new problems. Are the solutions for the rich more difficult to find than they are for the poor? They're different, but in my humble opinion such is life, and to solve the problem of life is traditionally almost impossible.'

Gloria apologised to her friends for 'preaching' about money.

'I can't stop myself,' she said. 'The fact of the matter is that money's an interesting subject for everybody everywhere. Is it less painful to talk about money if you have more rather than

225

less? I was a thrifty spinster before I was a multimillionairess. I had my nest-egg – or do I mean my mattress to fall on? – I was a miniature capitalist in the good or bad old days. And I worked at keeping my money intact, ready for rainy days. My investments were my blessings, and I thanked my God for them, they were compensation for my back, my spine. There's nothing wrong with money – I know that's a truism, but the point of truisms is that they're true. I've always liked it, personally, which is not to love it. I haven't done anything wonderful by giving some of my millions away, I've done the obvious thing, and had the great pleasure of seeing that it's been useful. My inheritance has enabled me to indulge myself without harming anybody.'

One of the congregation that heard Gloria 'preach' in spite of herself was Mr Chimbley. Their association had developed, and he took tea at The Wedge on numerous occasions. He had ventured to express sympathy for her disability, and she had been touched and explained it without inhibitions: that it was her cross, that her misshapenness had shaped her whole life and that it could have been worse. In winter the coal fire in the grate, the soft lighting of the sitting-room, the smile of his hostess as she offered him another slice of walnut cake, all conspired to make him more personal than he had ever before been with a client.

One afternoon he said to her: 'Your luck has also been mine, Miss Thwaite. I do not have many friends, and I feel that you and I have much in common, not least since neither of us have children.'

'Alas!'

'Yes – I suppose so,' he said.

'I pined to be a mother for some forty years.'

'Indeed?'

'Disappointment's a good school, it teaches you never to look over your shoulder.'

'Ah yes!'

'But you're a married man, Mr Chimbley.'

'I am ... But ... But my wife ... She has had poor health.'

'What a pity!'

'I have no complaints. Heather's been a good wife to me. I was not a romantic type.'

'Then a chasm opens between us, dear Mr Chimbley. I pined not only for children for all those years. But there it is! And here I am, and I can still smile.'

'Your millions, and how you have spent them, must be a satisfaction. You have won gratitude galore and, if I may say so, affection, which you deserve.'

'I know. I don't say "I know" complacently. It worries me sometimes that my life has turned out better than I could have believed for much of it – and so much better than for many handicapped people. I've compared money to a whole range of things. I think my most accurate comparison would be to water, because money like water supports life, and also finds the cracks and crannies, and brings rot and damage in its wake. You have to treat it with such care. I fear I may have failed to protect myself from the harm it can do.'

'I can't imagine any harm will befall you. I shall do my level best to see that it keeps its distance, provided that I am around to be of service.'

'Thank you, Mr Chimbley. Nevertheless I remember those other heirs and heiresses.'

'You are above them, Miss Thwaite – nothing that happened to them could possibly happen to you.'

'You're very kind,' she said.

Round about this time, Gloria fell down her stairs at The Wedge. She must have fallen on her way up to bed, she was fully dressed when she was found in a heap in her entrance hall in the morning. She was unconscious and icy cold. Janet Wolsey, who had done an hour's cleaning for Gloria twice a week for donkey's years, found her, covered her with a blanket, and rang 999 for an ambulance. The ambulance men confirmed that she was still alive, and removed her to the Intensive Care Ward at the NHS hospital in Teasham. She did not regain consciousness for a fortnight.

Her injuries were multiple but not life-threatening – she had a broken hip, a broken collarbone, bad bruising, especially to her head, and her speech was affected. She had not had a stroke. Her brain had been displaced and suffered trauma, and whether or not it would heal itself was in the lap of the gods. She had lost the power to communicate temporarily or for ever, but not her mind.

Her physical revival was tragic. At least the medical staff realised that she was not happy to be alive. She waved away pills and food, she tried to climb out of a window, and repeatedly to escape from the hospital. But her friends and beneficiaries gathered at her bedside and celebrated her recovery with congratulations and flowers, while she shook her head and eventually lay back defeated.

Mr Chimbley was concerned and pro-active in the matter of his client's complete recovery and her convalescence. He felt that he was authorised – and he assumed authority – to harass her doctors and order specialists in Harley Street to come down and examine her. When he told the invalid that he was getting her taken up to London in a private ambulance to undergo more tests and investigations, she covered her eyes with her hands and mouthed a word frantically, probably 'No!' He smiled at these antics and said she would be pleased when he had restored her to her old true self. He was even proud to tell her he was spending several hundred thousands of her remaining pounds on brain surgeons and the like. At a certain moment, after yet another disagreement with the NHS, he decided to move her into a private nursing home in a converted stately mansion.

Money again came to the fore in Gloria's chequered story. She had run out of it. Mr Chimbley had spent the relatively smallish residue of her capital, her nest egg and Shadrach's money, on the best and most expensive care and medical attention it could buy. But he was not in the mood to be frustrated. He put Goose Farm up for sale. Miss Thwaite had been on the point of offering it to families for holidays, to carers for respite, to battered wives, to children 'orphaned' by divorce, and her long list of dear unfortunates. Mr Chimbley called a halt to all of that. He sold it for getting on for a million, and paid out tens of thousands of pounds to keep Gloria just about ticking over. The expenditure went against the grain of his character and training; but he gritted his teeth as he signed the cheques and was pleased to feel unselfish for the first time.

Gloria's final eighteen months were very sad. She was not allowed to die, and her eyes that had twinkled were always full of tears. Shadrach's blessing or curse caught her out. Mr Chimbley's final note of fee soaked up the rest of the Goose Farm proceeds.